CRASH AND BURN!

They were down for good now, speeding across the grassy field at fifty knots an hour. Frank worked the brakes to slow the plane. Then it was as if the plane slammed into a brick wall.

Frank felt himself crushed against his seat belt, and the sound of tearing, wrenching metal filled the cockpit. The windshield imploded, showering Frank and Callie with shards of glass and a wet rush of churned, loose earth.

Then there was silence. Frank shook his head, trying to clear the dirt and glass away from his face. He realized the plane had flipped onto its back. He tried his door—no good.

Clear liquid ran down his face, burning his eyes. "Gasoline," he said, but no one answered. "The fuel tanks have ruptured," he said as loudly as he could. It felt as if his ribs were broken. His voice was barely a whisper. "We've got to get out of here," he said.

No one answered. . . .

Books in THE HARDY BOYS CASEFILES™ Series

#1 DEAD ON TARGET
#2 EVIL, INC.
#3 CULT OF CRIME
#4 THE LAZARUS PLOT
#5 EDGE OF DESTRUCTION
#6 THE CROWNING TERROR
#7 DEATHGAME
#8 SEE NO EVIL
#9 THE GENIUS THIEVES
#12 PERFECT GETAWAY
#13 THE BORGIA DAGGER
#14 TOO MANY TRAITORS
#29 THICK AS THIEVES
#30 THE DEADLIEST DARE
#32 BLOOD MONEY
#33 COLLISION COURSE
#35 THE DEAD SEASON
#37 DANGER ZONE
#41 HIGHWAY ROBBERY
#42 THE LAST LAUGH
#44 CASTLE FEAR
#45 IN SELF-DEFENSE
#46 FOUL PLAY
#47 FLIGHT INTO DANGER
#48 ROCK 'N' REVENGE
#49 DIRTY DEEDS
#50 POWER PLAY
#52 UNCIVIL WAR
#53 WEB OF HORROR
#54 DEEP TROUBLE
#55 BEYOND THE LAW
#56 HEIGHT OF DANGER
#57 TERROR ON TRACK
#60 DEADFALL
#61 GRAVE DANGER
#62 FINAL GAMBIT
#63 COLD SWEAT
#64 ENDANGERED SPECIES
#65 NO MERCY
#66 THE PHOENIX EQUATION
#69 MAYHEM IN MOTION
#70 RIGGED FOR REVENGE
#71 REAL HORROR
#73 BAD RAP
#74 ROAD PIRATES
#75 NO WAY OUT
#76 TAGGED FOR TERROR
#77 SURVIVAL RUN
#78 THE PACIFIC CONSPIRACY
#79 DANGER UNLIMITED
#80 DEAD OF NIGHT
#81 SHEER TERROR
#82 POISONED PARADISE
#83 TOXIC REVENGE
#84 FALSE ALARM
#85 WINNER TAKE ALL
#86 VIRTUAL VILLAINY
#87 DEAD MAN IN DEADWOOD
#88 INFERNO OF FEAR
#89 DARKNESS FALLS
#90 DEADLY ENGAGEMENT
#91 HOT WHEELS
#92 SABOTAGE AT SEA
#93 MISSION: MAYHEM
#94 A TASTE FOR TERROR
#95 ILLEGAL PROCEDURE
#96 AGAINST ALL ODDS
#97 PURE EVIL
#98 MURDER BY MAGIC
#99 FRAME-UP
#100 TRUE THRILLER
#101 PEAK OF DANGER
#102 WRONG SIDE OF THE LAW
#103 CAMPAIGN OF CRIME
#104 WILD WHEELS
#105 LAW OF THE JUNGLE
#106 SHOCK JOCK
#107 FAST BREAK
#108 BLOWN AWAY
#109 MOMENT OF TRUTH
#115 CAVE TRAP
#116 ACTING UP
#117 BLOOD SPORT
#118 THE LAST LEAP
#119 THE EMPEROR'S SHIELD
#120 SURVIVAL OF THE FITTEST
#121 ABSOLUTE ZERO
#122 RIVER RATS
#123 HIGH-WIRE ACT
#124 THE VIKING'S REVENGE
#125 STRESS POINT
#126 FIRE IN THE SKY

FIRE IN THE SKY

FRANKLIN W. DIXON

AN ARCHWAY PAPERBACK
Published by POCKET BOOKS
New York London Toronto Sydney Tokyo Singapore

AN ARCHWAY PAPERBACK *Original*

An Archway Paperback published by
POCKET BOOKS, a division of Simon & Schuster Inc.
1230 Avenue of the Americas, New York, NY 10020

Produced by Mega-Books Inc.

ISBN: 0-671-56125-1

First Archway Paperback printing November 1997

10 9 8 7 6 5 4 3 2 1

Printed in the U.S.A.

IL 6+

FIRE IN THE SKY

Chapter 1

JOE HARDY BARRELED UP the driveway of Vanessa Bender's farm in his mom's late-model sedan. His brother Frank's girlfriend, Callie Shaw, braced herself against the center armrest as the car skidded sideways, shooting up a rooster tail of dust and gravel. They lurched to a halt in front of the white clapboard house.

Joe hopped out and yelled up at the front porch, "Hurry up, Vanessa. Frank needs us at the airport. Now!"

Vanessa came bounding down the steps seconds later and jumped in the backseat. Joe hit the accelerator and they had backed halfway down the driveway by the time Vanessa had her door shut.

No one said anything for a few minutes. Callie kept tugging at loose strands of her blond hair and tucking them behind her ears.

"Okay, guys," Vanessa finally said. "What's going on? Joe driving like a maniac doesn't surprise me, but when you start fidgeting with your hair like that, Callie, I know something's wrong."

"It's probably nothing," Joe said.

Callie turned in her seat to face Vanessa. "Frank could be in trouble," she said.

Vanessa sat up straight. "What kind of trouble?"

"He called a little while ago," Joe said. "He said he was onto something big. Then he got cut off."

Vanessa looked at Joe. "What was he doing at the airport?" she asked.

"Renting a plane to go up for a couple of hours for some practice." They passed a sign that read Bayport Airport One Mile.

"Have you told your dad?" Callie asked, referring to Fenton Hardy, the brothers' father, who was a retired New York City Police detective and renowned private investigator.

"He's out of the country on a case," Joe said. "Besides, like I said, there's probably nothing to worry about."

"I hope you're right," Callie said. She twisted a strand of hair around her index finger and stared out the window.

Joe slowed as they pulled into the airport parking lot. It was after school on a beautiful early fall afternoon with plenty of sunshine still. The leaves were just starting to turn colors.

"Look," Vanessa called. "There's your van."

Joe parked the sedan a few rows behind the familiar black van, and the three teenagers got out quickly. Coming up quietly behind the van, Joe cupped his hands over his eyes and peeked in one of the tinted rear windows. "Nothing," he said. "Let's check the terminal."

"Hold it," Vanessa said from in front of the van. "Look at this."

Joe and Callie watched as Vanessa lifted a piece of paper from under the driver's side windshield wiper and unfolded it.

"What's it say?" Callie asked.

Vanessa read aloud: " 'J.H.: Am pursuing possible contraband evidence. Need backup.' " Vanessa stared at the note for a second longer, then handed it to Joe. It was written in awkward block letters. "J.H. is obviously you," she said. "It's signed 'HBC.' Who's that?"

"Why would Frank leave a note like that?" Callie asked. "And *where* is he pursuing evidence?"

"I have no idea," Joe said, crumpling the note into his pocket. "It doesn't even look like Frank's handwriting."

"The note mentions contraband," Callie said.

"Maybe we should check with some of the cargo handlers or look around the customs warehouse."

"Good idea," Joe replied.

"What if it's a trap?" Vanessa said.

"There's always that possibility," Joe said. "Let's just be extra careful."

Callie took the lead, quickly crossing the parking lot and skirting the awning around the front of the passenger terminal. The three teenagers stayed close to the long, brick building. Rounding a corner, they came to the eight-foot-high chain link fence surrounding the runway. A sign read Authorized Personnel Only. Behind the fence they could see a small passenger jet parked at a jetway. Its engines were hissing and whirring at idle, heat shimmering out behind them. Down to the left, set back from the runway, was a row of low green buildings—small hangars, warehouses, and offices.

Joe turned back to study the terminal. There were rows of rectangular smoked-glass windows lining the back of the building so people could watch as their loved ones boarded airplanes and lifted off into the cloudless sky.

Callie took in the scene. "There's no way to sneak in through the fence. We'll just have to figure a way in through the terminal building."

They hurried back to the main entrance. The double glass doors hissed open, and they strode in. Joe hung back, letting Callie and Vanessa go ahead. He watched as they turned to the right, heading away from the nearest ticket counter. There was a group of about twenty-five people sitting in the waiting area near the baggage carousel. Strangely, they were all turned away from the entrance.

As the girls passed the baggage claim area, the entire group suddenly leaped up, turned around, and shouted, "Surprise!" Callie shrieked, and Vanessa turned to face the noise, instinctively bracing herself for a fight.

Joe ran over to join the group just as they all yelled, "Happy Birthday, Callie!" in unison, blew streamers, and threw confetti all over her.

Callie held her hands to her gaping mouth in shock. A cloud of confetti settled silently around her, shiny little pieces of foil landing on her shoulders and in her hair. Frank Hardy stepped forward, grinning and holding a sign with "Happy Birthday, Callie" written out in big, bold letters.

Vanessa looked surprised at first, then marched over to Joe and gave him a shove on the shoulder.

"You creep," she said. "How could you let us think Frank was in trouble like that?"

"Hold it," Joe said with a chuckle, rubbing his shoulder. "It was all Frank's idea. I was just playing my part. That fake note was signed 'HBC'—Happy Birthday, Callie. Get it?"

"Yeah, I get it. But why didn't you clue me in

about the surprise? And don't say it was because I'd tell," Vanessa said.

"Okay, I won't say it." Joe grinned at her.

Once she recovered from her shock, Callie took the whole thing in stride, even chiding Joe about his acting skills. "I should have known something was up when you were so casual about that note. Then you let us lead the way with you following," she said. "It *was* all a trap. A Hardy trap."

Frank couldn't stop beaming at how well they'd taken the bait. Callie's friends hung around for only a half hour because the next day was a school day. They all joked and chatted and ate a birthday cake supplied by Chet Morton. The crowd thinned, and when only the four of them were left, Frank announced that Callie's present from him would be a trip to Loon Lake in the Adirondack Mountains for the long Columbus Day weekend. They would fly up to do some hiking and canoeing and enjoy the fall foliage at its best.

"That sounds fantastic," Callie said. "I can't wait."

"Well, we don't have to wait to check out the plane," Frank said. "How about we take a ride over Bayport?"

"Right now?" Callie asked. "Isn't it going to get dark soon?"

"It'll just be a quick flight," Frank said.

"Maybe we'll see the lights go on all over Bayport. Follow me."

After passing through security, Frank led the other three out onto the runway to a square-shaped building, the front section of which was constructed almost entirely of glass. They could see several rows of planes lined up precisely inside this area.

"Wow," Callie said, looking up. "It's like a showroom. There must be fifteen jets in there."

"This is Starkey Aviation," Frank said, opening the front door. "I've rented planes from them before. Wait here just a minute."

Frank quickly disappeared into an office and was back in a flash. Within minutes, a friendly, rotund mechanic had towed a single-engine prop plane from the back of the hangar and Frank had completed his preflight inspection.

The four teens climbed aboard. Callie took the copilot's seat next to Frank, while Joe and Vanessa took the two backseats.

"Okay, let's buckle up," Frank said as he began to run through his checklist. He started the engine, checked all the switches, dials, and controls and then motioned for Vanessa to lean forward to watch him steer the plane toward the runway. As he eased off on the brakes and gave it some gas, the little plane surged forward and started bumping down the taxiway.

"The tops of the rudder pedals control the

brakes," he shouted over the buzz of the engine. "It's simple. You just push harder on the side you want to turn to." He demonstrated by pushing his left foot into the top of the left rudder pedal and lifting off with his right foot. The plane swung neatly around, and suddenly they were facing the runway.

Vanessa gave Joe the thumbs-up sign.

"Everybody ready?" Frank yelled over his shoulder. They all nodded, and he spoke into the radio. "Starkey four-one-three-seven ready for takeoff, runway seven eastbound departure."

The radio squawked with static before the tower answered: "Starkey four-one-three-seven, contact Bayport departure seven east cleared for takeoff."

With one hand, Frank switched the fuel mixture to full rich, then smoothly pulled the throttle knob all the way out. The howl of the prop grew louder and louder as he carefully built up speed. When the air speed indicator read 55 knots, Frank started pulling back on the yoke. The plane seemed to do a little leap into the air. Air currents rocked and jolted it like a boat, but soon they were up into smoother air and cruising nicely.

The radio crackled to life. "Starkey three-niner-niner November India, radar contact, say altitude."

"Climbing to one thousand feet, Starkey three-niner-niner November India," Frank answered. "Contact Bayport departure one-two-seven-zero."

"Roger, one-two-seven-zero. So long, Starkey three-niner-niner November India."

"I just love how peaceful it is up here," Callie said after the radio went silent.

"Hey, Frank," Vanessa yelled over the roar of the engine. "How about showing us some maneuvers?"

"You got it." Frank said something into the radio they couldn't hear, then steered the plane away from the airport and out over some beautiful stretches of woods and farmland to the north and east of Bayport.

"What's up?" Callie asked.

Rather than answer with words, Frank turned the control yoke to the left. The plane began to bank in that direction.

"Vanessa," Frank said. "The wheel controls the ailerons on the wings. But notice how I push on the left rudder pedal, too. Rudder deflection keeps the nose pointed in the right direction."

Vanessa nodded. Frank showed her a few more banks and climbs before they headed back toward the airport.

"Hey, there's my house," Vanessa called out. They all looked out and saw the Benders' farmhouse, flanked by its neat red barn, about three miles downwind and three thousand feet below.

The plots of land around the farm were laid out in perfect squares, with rows of trees separating each section.

Frank started to say something, then wrinkled his nose. "What's that smell?" he said to himself. He immediately turned his attention to the instrument panel. "Smells like gasoline."

The plane bucked once like an angry bronco. Frank grabbed the yoke with both hands, trying to maintain control. Again, there was a jolt, and the plane shuddered in the air. Joe glanced up at Frank a little uncomfortably. The next thing he noticed was a tomblike silence in the cockpit. The engine had stalled.

Frank checked the throttle knob, then the carburetor heat. Everything was in the right place, but the oil temperature needle was rising fast. The batteries were okay, so he switched off the power with the ignition key, then switched it back on, trying to restart the engine. It coughed and sputtered, then sent a violent rattling and shaking down the length of the fuselage.

Next Frank noticed the oil temperature needle was headed right off the scale. A red warning light came on with a buzz. This was no time to panic.

The plane shook violently again, four or five big hiccups that made all three passengers grab for their seats. Frank shut down the engine. There was something seriously wrong.

"What's going on?" Vanessa said. Her face had gone pale.

Frank radioed the Bayport tower and, speaking quickly and calmly into the microphone, advised them of the situation.

"We're going to have to do an emergency landing," Joe said. "There's no way we can make it back to the airport."

Frank worked the controls, deftly keeping the plane as straight and level as possible as they dropped—half-gliding, half-falling—out of the sky. There was a two-lane highway, probably County Road 518 by Frank's reckoning, about two miles across the farmland, but they were coming down too fast to make it.

"I'm going to get us to that field over there," he said, nodding out his window at a long, flat space full of ruts where crops had been harvested. He banked left, letting the plane pick up speed.

Frank moved the flap switch down to the ten-degree position. He pulled back on the stick, trying to bring the nose up as they careened toward the ground. He flew by touch, turning back into the wind and adding more angle to the flaps.

They were less than one hundred feet off the ground now. Frank coasted the rocking plane over a row of trees.

"You've only got a few hundred yards," Joe said.

"Easy does it," Frank said, his jaw clenched in concentration. "Hang on, everybody; it might be a little bumpy in the dirt." The next row of trees loomed in the distance.

Callie gripped both sides of her seat and tried not to look out her window.

Holding the yoke steady, Frank waited to feel the sensation of the wheels touching the rough ground. Their airspeed was over sixty knots, approaching seventy miles per hour.

The plane hit and bounced up, then hit again.

"That's it," Joe said. "You got it."

They were down for good now, and Frank worked the brakes to slow them down. He concentrated on keeping the pressure equal on both main wheels. There was a lot of bouncing along the ruts, but Frank seemed to have it under control.

Then it was as if the plane slammed into a brick wall.

Frank felt himself crushed against his seat belt, and the sound of tearing, wrenching metal filled the cockpit. For a second Frank felt weightless, as if he'd been lifted out of his seat by a giant, powerful hand. Were they airborne again? A gut-wrenching impact shattered that thought. The windshield imploded, showering Frank and Callie with shards of glass and a wet rush of churned, loose earth.

Then there was silence. They were stopped.

Frank shook his head, trying to clear the dirt and glass from his face. He realized the plane had flipped over onto its back. He tried his door—no good.

Clear liquid ran down his face, burning his eyes. "Gasoline," he said out loud, but no one answered. "We've got a ruptured fuel tank," he said as loudly as he could. It felt as if his ribs were broken. His voice was barely a whisper. "We've got to get out of here, and fast," he said.

No one answered.

Chapter 2

FRANK HEARD A BUZZING SOUND from somewhere deep in the instrument panel. Off and on, off and on; it sounded like a fly caught in a jar. He knew right away what it meant—electrical wires shorting against one another. If the sparks ignited the leaking fuel, they would be toast.

Hanging upside-down, Frank worked to unlatch his seat belt. "Joe," he said. "Callie, Vanessa."

"Frank."

It was Joe, his voice not much more than a croak.

The latch opened, and Frank tumbled out of his seat. "Joe," he said. "Are you okay?"

"I just had the wind knocked out of me. I think we're okay back here."

Pushing the loose dirt and glass aside, Frank managed to squeeze through the windshield opening. The smell of gas was getting stronger.

Frank rushed to the other side of the plane. He could see Callie inside, unconscious and bleeding from a deep wound in her forehead. "Oh, man," he said. "I think she forgot her seat belt."

Within seconds Joe and Vanessa had scrambled free of the wreckage.

"Get help," Frank said, pointing in the direction of the highway. "Callie's in bad shape."

Vanessa looked shaken, her face streaked with dirt and blood, but she quickly pulled herself together. "I'll try to flag someone down," she said, heading toward the road.

Joe knelt down to help Frank clear the debris from around the door frame.

"I don't think she's breathing," Frank said, reaching in through the open door and lightly pressing a finger to his girlfriend's neck. "I can't find a pulse."

"Be careful moving her," Joe said. "Her neck could be broken." Working together, the two brothers slowly pulled Callie free.

The tiny plane was on its back like a dead bird, its landing gear pointed up at the sky. A thin plume of dark smoke began to curl out of the engine compartment. "Let's move her toward the road," Joe said. "This thing could blow any second."

"We don't have time, Joe." They were only a few yards from the smoldering wreckage. "I've got to try CPR."

Frank exhaled two quick breaths into Callie's mouth to inflate her lungs. Then he started chest compressions.

Joe hurried back to the plane and crawled back in through the passenger door. Inside, roiling smoke was starting to fill the compartment. He had to feel his way along the wall, but finally he found the fire extinguisher. He held his shirt tail over his mouth to keep from choking and scrambled back out of the plane.

The engine compartment burst into flames as he rushed up to it, the heat sending him reeling back. He squeezed the trigger on the extinguisher, sending a jet of white foam toward the base of the flames. He stepped in closer, fighting the heat.

Joe sprayed until the canister went dry. Then he carefully checked the engine. It looked as if the fire was out. He dropped the extinguisher and rushed back to help Frank.

They could hear sirens in the distance.

"We're running out of time," Frank said. "She probably stopped breathing when the plane flipped."

After five or six more cycles of compressions and breathing, Frank checked for a pulse. He felt a weak flutter. "Got to keep it up," he said. The sirens were closer now, but Callie's lips were turning blue—she needed oxygen. "Come on, Callie," Frank said. "Hang in there. Just take one breath, one breath at a time."

An ambulance came tearing across the rutted field, lights flashing, siren blaring. Two burly paramedics bounded out the back doors before the driver had even stopped.

Joe had to drag his brother away to let the medics work. "Come on, Frank," he said. "They need room to work."

A fire truck from the airport arrived next, and as two men in metallic, fireproof jumpsuits sprayed foam on the smoldering plane, another firefighter tried to lead the Hardys away.

"We're not going anywhere," Frank said firmly.

At that moment one of the paramedics looked up and said, "She's breathing on her own. We've got to transport her now."

Frank stepped forward, ignoring the firefighter. "I'm going with you."

"All right, all right, everyone goes to the hospital," the firefighter said. "They'll have to check you out, too. You can find out about the girl's condition when you get there."

Another firefighter came up, pulling the protective mask from his face. He wasn't as friendly as the first guy. "I need everybody's name," he said. "There's obviously going to be an investigation."

Joe was back at Bayport Hospital at four-thirty the next morning. He'd spent a lot of the previous evening getting poked and prodded by doctors and grilled by an investigator from the National Transportation Safety Board. Everyone had checked out okay except Callie, and Frank had stayed at the hospital all night to be with her.

Joe found his brother sacked out in a chair outside the intensive care unit. Deciding to let Frank sleep a few more minutes, he quietly took a seat next to him. About twenty minutes later Frank stirred, slowly opened his eyes, and stood up and stretched. His normally neat wavy brown hair was tangled and he had dark circles under his eyes. He rubbed his hands over them and said, "Did you bring coffee?"

"Sure did," Joe replied. "Coffee and doughnuts. I guess if you're hungry that means Callie's okay, right?"

Frank tore the plastic lid off his coffee and took a big gulp without adding cream or sugar. He winced but seemed to want to burn away the memory of the previous afternoon's events. "She had a rough night." Frank took another gulp, the steam clouding his face from view for a second, and continued. "She's got broken ribs, a punctured lung, a fractured skull—"

"A skull fracture," Joe said. "How serious?"

"That's what kept us up all night," Frank said. "The doctors were concerned her brain might swell, so they drilled a hole in her skull to relieve the pressure. She's got a tube to drain out the extra fluid." Frank shook his head, then glanced at his watch. "A couple of hours ago she woke up and talked—that means the worst part is over."

"Are her mom and dad here?"

"They just went home to get some rest." Frank drained his coffee cup, then turned it slowly in his hands, studying it. His face seemed to harden. "We've got to find out what happened, Joe. Callie almost died in that crash."

Joe stood up. "Let's do it. Let's head out to the crash site and see what we can turn up."

After giving the nurse their cellular phone number and instructions to call with any change in Callie's condition, the Hardys hurried out to their van. Joe drove while Frank tried to run a comb through his hair.

"What do you think happened?" Joe asked.

"I told that investigator, what was his name?"

"Hutchens," Joe said. "Bryan Hutchens."

"I told Hutchens everything I could remember. It was strange, though. I've never had that kind of trouble with an engine before. Usually if it stalls you can just glide down nice and easy. This thing was almost impossible to control."

"Could it have been turbulence on the way down?"

"No way. I think something came loose in the engine compartment. When I restarted it, it almost shook itself apart."

"If only we could've made it to the road," Joe noted. "We could have had a nice, smooth landing."

"I tried," Frank said. "I thought I had it. And it wasn't a bad landing."

"Until we flipped over."

"Right, but I remember being extra careful with the brakes. I didn't want one wheel to lock up and send us out of control."

"Maybe they've already found the problem," Joe said.

The sun was just peeking over the horizon when the brothers arrived at the crash site. The barren field and the reddish purple light made the scene look as if it were taking place on the moon. Pieces of the plane were strewn over a quarter-mile-long path, from where Frank had first touched down to where the plane had finally flipped over and stopped. Airport security had cordoned off the area with wooden stakes and red tape, and four or five people were moving quietly in and out of the long shadows cast by the rising sun. They all carried clipboards and seemed to be surveying the area, mapping where each piece of the plane had ended up.

Joe parked the van behind a white government sedan and the two brothers got out. No one seemed to notice as they ducked under the tape and walked toward the body of the plane.

"Wow, there's not much left," Frank whispered.

"Yeah. Looks like more of it burned than I thought," Joe replied. "I guess we were lucky."

A man in black coveralls stood by the front of the plane, shining a flashlight in on the instrument panel. He turned as the Hardys approached.

"Hold it right there," he said, his sharp voice piercing the eerie silence. "This area is off limits."

It was Bryan Hutchens, the National Transportation Safety Board investigator. His black baseball cap had the letters NTSB in gold over the bill. He was middle-aged, with slightly hunched shoulders, as if he were carrying an invisible weight on his back, and sharp, well-defined features with a focused expression. He looked like the kind of person who wouldn't let a single detail get past him.

Frank held out his hand. The man hesitated for a moment, then shook it. "What are you doing here?" he asked suspiciously.

"We just wanted to see if you've come up with anything yet."

The man withdrew his hand quickly. "Unless you have some more details to add to your account of the crash, you've got no business being here."

"No. I told you everything," Frank said.

"We might be able to lend a hand," Joe offered.

"Absolutely not," the man said, starting to turn back to the wreckage. "I got enough people looking over my shoulder already. And I can't have you two tampering. Now clear out."

Frank put his hand on the man's arm. "I need to find out what happened up there."

Hutchens twisted free from Frank. "That's my job, so get your hand off me and let me do it."

"It's been over twelve hours," Joe said, trying to catch a glimpse into the engine compartment. "You must have something."

"Listen," Hutchens said, pointing his clipboard at Frank. "You two had better cool it or I'll have you arrested. *I* will determine the cause of this crash, and I'll do it without your interference."

"We're entitled to some information and a fair investigation," Frank said, glaring at Hutchens.

"All right then, how about *this,* smart aleck?" Hutchens said. "Ninety-nine percent of these incidents are pilot error, so I'm temporarily suspending your license."

"What? You can't do that."

"Yes, I can. And get used to it, because as soon as I find a shred of evidence for pilot error the suspension becomes permanent."

Frank's face reddened. "Hey, I'm an experienced pilot," he said. "This airplane had a serious mechanical failure. All you're trying to do is sew up this investigation the easy way. Blame the pilot, ground him, and close the file."

Hutchens took a step toward Frank and growled, "That's enough out of you." He glared at Joe, then back at Frank. "You turn right around and go home—now. And consider yourself lucky that pretty little girlfriend of yours didn't die. Because if she did, you'd be facing even more serious charges."

Something in Frank snapped. He grabbed the front of Hutchens's coveralls, shook hard, and yelled, "How dare you accuse me!"

Chapter 3

JOE STEPPED IN QUICKLY and pried the two of them apart like a referee separating two brawling hockey players. Frank tried to reach past Joe's shoulder to grab at Hutchens, but Joe planted a forearm firmly across his brother's chest, holding him back.

Hutchens shook himself loose and went back to the overturned plane.

"You think I tried to kill my girlfriend?" Frank shouted. "That's ridiculous."

"I go where the evidence leads me," Hutchens called over his shoulder. "You'll get your temporary suspension in the mail tomorrow."

"That's a mistake," Frank said. He took a deep breath, working to regain his composure.

"Is that a threat?" Hutchens shot back.

"Just the truth," Frank said. "In case it matters at all in your investigation."

"For the last time, clear out and let me do my job," Hutchens said. He was shining his flashlight around inside the passenger compartment. "You'll be the first to know what I determine, believe me."

Joe turned and beckoned for Frank to follow him. They both knew it was time to take Hutchens's advice and leave. Frank stalked past Joe and back to the van in silence. On the way home, he just stared out the window.

"You okay?" Joe asked as they drove through the downtown area.

"Yeah, I'm fine," Frank said. "I guess I just lost my cool when he said what he said about Callie. I just can't stand not being in on the investigation—and leaving it up to somebody like Hutchens."

It was going to be another beautiful, crisp early-fall day, and the city of Bayport was just starting to wake up. Men and women in suits headed into office buildings, newspapers tucked under their arms. At one corner a man in green coveralls hosed down the sidewalk in front of a gas station.

"So I guess you don't trust Hutchens," Joe said.

"Brilliant deduction," Frank said, realizing Joe was still in shock over how he'd vented his anger at the NTSB man. "Aside from his lousy attitude, I think we should keep an eye on him."

By the time Joe turned the van into the high school parking lot, Frank had figured out their next step.

"Here's the plan," he announced. "Tonight we go back to the airport. There's an NTSB hangar there, which is where they'll store the wreckage."

"And we do our own inspection," Joe added.

"Exactly."

"I'll talk to Phil before chemistry class and see if he can join us," Joe said. Phil Cohen was the Hardys' good friend and Bayport High School's resident technological guru. "Whatever went wrong with that plane, the three of us should be able to figure it out."

It was close to midnight by the time Frank switched off the lights and engine of the van and coasted into the airport parking lot. A half-moon threw a gauzy, silver light across the terminal building and hangars in the distance.

Joe pulled a pair of night-vision binoculars from his pack. In order to let in enough light, the lenses were as big around as softballs. "I don't see any movement," he said, scanning the area. "My guess is that the NTSB hangar is that rectangular building with no signs on it."

"That's it," Phil said, poking his head out from the darkness in the back of the van. He held a flashlight in one hand and a portable socket set in the other.

"Let's go—quietly," Frank said.

Joe led the way along the fence, far from the passenger terminal. Bayport Airport wasn't busy enough to schedule late-night flights, but the boys had no idea who might still be around.

After boosting Phil over the fence, Frank and Joe followed. They passed the Starkey Aviation hangar. "Wow," Phil said. At night, the building was even more spectacular than during the day. A thin lattice of black marble surrounded huge, thirty-foot-square panes of sparkling plate glass. Dim lights high in the ceiling glimmered off the twelve or fifteen prop planes and private jets parked inside.

Up ahead, Joe had reached the NTSB hangar. A dented steel door and a few small windows were the only breaks in the vast metal wall. A shade covered most of the window next to the door.

"Look at this," Joe whispered.

"I don't see anything," Phil said, standing on his toes to peer in the window.

"Just a second, you will."

Just then a beam of yellow light filtered around the edges of the blind, then disappeared.

"Someone's in there snooping around with a flashlight," Frank said.

"So what do we do?" Phil asked. "Wait?"

"We go in," Joe answered, pulling his set of lock picks from his back pocket.

Working quickly and quietly, Joe had the door open in less than a minute. The three of them slipped into the hangar and stood frozen against the wall, letting their eyes adjust to the inside darkness.

The remains of the plane sat in a heap in the center of the vast cement floor. Frank could see the shadowy outline of someone working on the wreck. The knocks and taps of the tools the person was using echoed off the walls and ceiling. It was like watching a cockroach nibble on a crumb on the kitchen floor: All Frank wanted to do was flip on the lights and squash this creep for good.

Making a circling motion with his hands, Joe signaled Frank and Phil to spread out and surround the figure. Frank nodded and pointed Phil in the right direction. If they could come up on this guy from three directions, they'd have him trapped.

Frank waited a solid minute, counting silently to himself. Once he was certain Joe and Phil were in place, he started toward the suspect.

He was no more than fifty feet away when he heard a loud metallic crash. Frank froze. The figure straightened up and clicked off his flashlight, plunging them all into total darkness.

Frank heard Joe shout, "Get him." Pulling his penlight from his pocket, Frank rushed forward. He and Joe got to the plane at the same time.

"He's gone," Joe said, panning the narrow

beam of his flashlight around. They heard a door slam at the far end of the hangar.

"He obviously knew his way around," Frank muttered.

Phil joined them; he was limping. "Sorry, guys," he moaned. "I think I tripped over a toolbox." He leaned over and pulled up the cuff of his jeans. A small trickle of blood zigzagged its way down his shinbone and into his sock.

Frank tried to hide his disappointment. "It's okay, Phil," he said. "I wonder who else is doing a little after-hours investigating."

"You think that was Hutchens?" Joe asked.

"Why would he run off?" Frank said. "He belongs here." He took the big, lantern-style flashlight from Phil and headed for the door. He played the light across the airfield, but saw no sign of anyone. "Long gone," he said to himself.

Back inside, he shined the light on the plane. It looked even worse inside than it had out in the field. The white paint was peeled off in big patches, revealing naked, torn, and dented aluminum. The left wing was shorn completely in half, exposing the ruptured fuel tank; the right wing drooped down, almost touching the floor. "Whoever was here was interested in the engine," Frank said. "Let's see what they were up to."

Joe reached into the engine compartment and felt around. "I could use some light over here," he said.

Frank brought the light close.

Phil let out a whistle. "I've never seen anything like that before."

"What?" Frank asked.

"Shine the light on the other side," Joe said. "Now back here, against the fire wall."

"You noticing what I'm noticing?" Phil asked.

"What is it?" Frank asked again.

"It's the engine mounts," Joe said, pointing to a *C*-shaped clamp deep in the recesses of the compartment. "There should be five of them to hold the engine to the frame—two on each side and one on the back."

"Right," Phil added, darting around Frank to get to the back of the engine compartment. "And look here. Two of them are missing, the back one and the one on Joe's side. And another one is broken. The bolts are sheared off inside the engine block."

"Oh, that's a big surprise," Frank said sarcastically. "Especially since the rest of the plane came through with barely a scratch."

"Broken engine mounts are one thing," Phil said. "But you've only got one of those. Missing mounts are something else. Where'd they go?"

Joe nodded in agreement. "I think our visitor was in the process of pulling all the mounts when we interrupted him."

"And look at this one," Phil said, trotting back over to Joe's side.

Frank zoomed the light in close.

"You're right, Phil," Joe said. "There's no grease on it or anything. It's brand-new."

"Here's what I figure," Phil said, looking at Frank intently. "One or two of the five engine mounts failed while you were flying around. Joe told me you smelled gas just before the engine quit, right?"

"Right."

"With two engine mounts gone, the torque from the prop must have been shaking that engine around inside the compartment like crazy. The fuel lines probably ripped right in half."

"But what about after the engine stalled?" Frank asked. "The plane kept shaking."

"The engine weighs almost five hundred pounds," Phil said. "In a plane this size, that's a lot of weight."

"Makes sense," Joe agreed. "With the engine halfway falling out, the controls weren't balanced anymore. It must've been like trying to fly a refrigerator."

"With the door open," Phil added.

"Good theory, good analogy, guys," Frank said. "Now let's see if we can find some hard evidence to prove it. And we should also check the brakes. That was really what got us almost killed—flipping over when we landed."

"Give me the nine-sixteenths socket," Joe said

to Phil. "Let's back these broken bolts out of the engine block and see what they look like."

"I'll check the landing gear," Frank said. Leaving Phil and his brother to work on the engine, Frank took the big flashlight and an Allen wrench and crawled as far under the wreckage as he could. He had to scrape away clods of dirt and grass, but he finally exposed the crumpled landing gear. He used the Allen wrench to remove the body panels around the gear struts. A good look at the hydraulic lines leading to the brakes would tell him something, he figured.

He was working to loosen a frozen bolt when all three of them heard a noise outside.

"What was that?" Phil asked nervously.

"Maybe our friend is back. I'll check it out," Joe whispered, shining his penlight toward the floor so it wouldn't expose his face.

"Hold on, Joe. I'll go with you." Frank struggled to get out from under the plane, but Joe had already disappeared into the darkness.

Once outside Joe felt exposed. The moon was like a giant spotlight shining right on him. He stayed close to the hangar wall, edging along in a half crouch.

Slowly rounding the corner of the building, Joe spotted a figure spying through a window. He figured the guy to be about his height and weight—six feet, 185. Whoever it was, it wasn't Hutchens.

"Hey," Joe yelled. "What are you doing here?"

The man turned. Joe couldn't make out his face.

"I asked you a question," Joe said, approaching.

Without warning, the man lowered his head and charged at Joe like an angry bull. He buried his skull in Joe's solar plexus, and the two of them went down hard. Joe's penlight clattered across the asphalt.

The man tried to pin Joe to the ground, but Joe gave him a quick jab to the throat with the first knuckle of his thumb. He felt the blow sink into the soft spot between the guy's collarbone. His attacker rolled off, coughing and gagging.

Joe sprang after him. The man was still bent over and Joe slugged him with an uppercut. The man reeled backward and fell to the ground.

Joe lost him in the darkness for a second, then spotted him trying to get up. One more good shot, he thought to himself, and this guy's out.

He stepped in, fist cocked. Something metallic flashed off to his left, then his ears were ringing, and he suddenly had the coppery taste of blood in his mouth.

Joe was trying to figure out what had happened when everything went black.

Chapter 4

THERE WAS THE MOON AGAIN. It swam slowly into focus through a sea of star-speckled black.

"Joe, buddy, are you okay?" It was Phil.

Phil's face and then Frank's came into view above him, bracketing the moon like two bookends.

Joe reached up with his hand and felt a knot growing over his left ear. "I got hit with something," he said, sitting up.

Frank helped him to his feet.

"Could this be the culprit?" Phil hefted an eighteen-inch section of lead pipe. "I found it lying a few feet away. He must've picked it up and cracked you over the head."

"That guy sure got lucky," Joe said. He shook

his head, clearing the cobwebs. "I was about to put him down for the count." He spat some blood on the ground. "He hit me so hard I bit my tongue."

"Get a good look at him?" Frank asked.

"No. The only thing I saw was his feet. He had on light-colored snakeskin cowboy boots. Believe me, I'll recognize them if I ever see them again." Joe hesitated for a moment.

"You dizzy?" Phil asked.

"No, I just thought of something else. A smell. His hair smelled like hair spray."

"That's good," Frank said. "We'll go around to every country and western joint in Bayport and ask about a guy in snakeskin boots wearing hair spray."

"You're almost funny, Frank." Joe turned back to the hangar. "Let's finish with the plane and get out of here before we run into any more lead pipes."

Back inside, Phil and Frank finished gathering the suspect parts from the landing gear and engine compartment while Joe searched the rest of the building. At one end he came to a row of small offices. He walked down the row until he came to one marked Bryan Hutchens, Investigator. With some coaxing from Joe's pick, the door popped open.

Except for furniture, the office was totally empty. At first Joe thought someone must have rifled through Hutchens's desk and cabinets, stealing all his files, but a closer examination seemed to confirm that Hutchens was either incredibly neat or just didn't have much work.

Joe opened every desk drawer. There was stationery with the National Transportation Safety Board letterhead; there were envelopes, pens, pencils, staples, and paper clips. The desk had everything a person would need for an office except files. The file cabinet was equally barren.

Frank poked his head in the door. "Find anything?"

"Nothing," Joe replied. "Other than routine inspections, I don't think Hutchens really does anything. Maybe you don't have to worry about your pilot's license after all."

"I'll believe that when I hear it from Hutchens's own mouth," Frank said.

"Well, there's nothing here. Grab Phil and let's go."

"I'm ready," Phil said, showing up behind Frank. He held up a brown paper bag. "I'll take these parts to the machine shop tomorrow for analysis."

"Good," Frank said. "And I think Joe and I should go by Starkey Aviation and look up the maintenance files on the plane."

When the Hardys walked into the Starkey Aviation hangar the next afternoon after school, the sunshine coming through the enormous panes of glass painted a gridwork of shadows and light across the rows of sparkling airplanes.

The mechanic who'd wheeled the plane out for them two days ago stood under an executive jet, bolting an access panel onto the underbelly. He was short and round and had a jolly pink face.

Frank introduced his brother to the man. "Joe, this is Opal."

"Opal?" Joe extended his hand.

The man shook his head silently, then held his hands out, palms up. They were covered with grease. "That's me all right." He walked over to a tool cabinet, pulled out a rag to wipe his hands, and came back. "I'm Opal Berkemeier," the man said. "But folks call me Buddy."

As they shook, Joe noticed the man's hands again. They were as broad as paper plates. "Nice to meet you, Opal, er, Buddy," he said.

"I'm chief mechanic around here," Buddy said, in his booming voice. "And your brother, if I'm not mistaken, is the son of a gun who did a back flip in one of my planes a couple days ago."

"That's sort of what we wanted to talk to you about," Joe said.

"Buddy!" A shrill voice filled the spacious hangar. "Buddy, don't forget you need to get that charter ready to go by four-thirty." A very attractive dark-haired young woman came out of an office across the hangar and strode toward them, her high heels clicking smartly on the cement.

Joe arched an eyebrow at his brother. "Who's that?" he said under his breath.

"Brenda Starkey," Frank whispered. "She rented me the plane. Her dad owns this place."

Buddy hurried back to work before Brenda could scold him anymore.

"Frank Hardy," Brenda said, loudly. "I've been meaning to call you. How's your girlfriend? Callie Shaw, right? Is she okay?"

"Yes, thanks," Frank said. "She's doing much better."

"We were so worried, you know. It was just terrible what happened. Would you like some coffee? A soda, maybe?"

Joe was about to say yes, but Frank shook his head. "No thanks," he said. "We just came by because we had a few questions about the plane."

"Sure, okay," Brenda said.

Joe found himself looking right into the young woman's eyes. In her heels she was very nearly as tall as he was. She wore an expensive-looking navy blue business suit with a white silk blouse.

"Is your dad around?" Frank asked.

"No, he's out of town on business." Brenda crossed her hands in front of her. "I pretty much take care of the day-to-day operations, so what can I do for you?"

Frank glanced over to where Buddy was checking the flaps on a twin-engine prop plane. "I'd like to see the maintenance records for our plane."

"I don't think that's possible." Brenda took a step toward Frank. "You understand with an investigation going on we can't bc handing out the files."

"We just want to try to figure out what went wrong," Frank replied. "How about just making copies of the maintenance log?"

Brenda's voice had an edge to it. "Hold it right there, Frank. Now, don't get me wrong. I want to find out what happened as much as you do. But we're preparing to hand everything over to the NTSB. Maybe if you have your lawyer give us a call we can work something out." She gave Frank a quick, insincere smile.

Frank started to say something, but Brenda pointed to the door. "If that's all maybe you'd better go."

"But—" Joe said, stepping in.

"No. I think that'll have to be all. I'm sorry." Brenda motioned politely but firmly for them to see themselves out.

Joe followed his brother. Once they were outside, though, he thought of something else. "Frank, what about who rented the plane before us?" he asked.

"What about them?"

"Maybe they had a problem, too. We can ask

them. If she won't let us see the maintenance records, she can at least tell us who had the plane before we did."

"She'll never give up that information."

"How about Buddy? He seemed like a friendly guy. I'll be right back." Joc ducked back into the hangar.

This time he didn't see Buddy anywhere. He peeked in Brenda's office window—the space was empty. This was his chance. He cracked the door and was about to sneak in, when he noticed a narrow wooden door marked Private at the back of the office. The door opened up, and a brown-haired young man about six feet tall started to step into the office.

Spotting Joe, the young man quickly retreated, closing the door behind him. "Hey," Joe said as he dashed across the room and tried the door. It was locked. He turned and ran back outside to where Frank was waiting.

"Frank. It was the same guy."

"What guy?"

"The guy with the cowboy boots who clocked me last night."

Chapter 5

"WHERE? INSIDE?"

Joe nodded and said, "He disappeared behind a closed door before I could stop him. Come on."

Joe led the way around the building to the row of windows behind the offices. Peeking in through the slats of the blinds, the Hardys saw Brenda Starkey and the young man standing in what looked like a small supply room. Shelves were stacked with boxes of parts and office supplies, and a copy machine sat against one wall.

Brenda and Joe's assailant were having a heated argument. The young man, especially, looked as if he was losing his cool.

Frank noticed the guy's perfectly styled and blow-dried hair. "He looks like Elvis Presley," he said.

"They're really going at it," Joe said. "Why don't we go in and surprise them?"

"Hold on. Here comes somebody else."

An older man with short gray hair entered the room. He was fit for his age and distinguished looking but seemed tired and worn down. He put a finger in the middle of the young man's chest and started in on him.

"That's John Starkey," Frank said.

The Hardys watched as the young man knocked the older man's hand away and said something to Brenda. She threw up her hands as if to say there was nothing she could do.

The young man said something more to John Starkey, then charged out of the room. Brenda chased after him.

"Let's do it, Frank," Joe said, tearing off toward the front of the building. "Elvis Presley there owes me an explanation."

The Hardys made it around the hangar just in time to see Brenda and the young man jump into a white foreign-made convertible and speed off.

Joe sprinted after the sports car for a few yards, then gave up. "We should've gone after them inside," he muttered, returning to the front of the hangar.

"At least we know the Elvis look-alike is connected to Starkey Aviation," Frank said. He watched the convertible streak through the gate and off airport property. "I have a feeling you'll get your chance to even the score, Joe."

"I can't wait."

Frank led the way back into the hangar. "Let's see what we can find out from Mr. Starkey," he said. "Mr. Starkey, who seems to have returned early from his business trip."

"Oh, that's right. Brenda said he was away on business. Why do you think she lied?" Joe asked.

"Probably so her father wouldn't have to deal with us."

"You think Starkey hired our cowboy friend there to cover up the cause of the accident?"

"Why else would he have been messing with the wreckage at the NTSB hangar last night?"

The door next to Brenda's office had a brass nameplate on it reading John Starkey, President. The Hardys barged in, startling a secretary seated at a desk in the outer office. "We're here to see Mr. Starkey," Joe announced.

Before the woman could do more than stand up in surprise, Frank and Joe had forced their way into the back office, where they found the gray-haired man sitting behind a desk, holding his head in his hands.

"Mr. Starkey," Frank said, "your daughter said you were out of town."

The man's head popped up. "Who are you?" he asked warily. "Are you from NTSB? No, you've rented planes from me before, haven't you?"

"He sure has," Joe said, glancing around the office. He noticed shelves of painstakingly constructed model airplanes—everything from WW I biplanes to modern supersonic fighters. "We're Frank and Joe Hardy."

The secretary had followed the Hardys in. She just stood there, not sure what to do.

The man stood up abruptly, his face reddening. "You're . . . you're the ones who're going to get me shut down for good. I can't talk to you."

"When was that plane last serviced?" Frank asked.

Starkey just shook his head. "Margorie," he said to his secretary. "Can you call someone to escort these two young men out?"

"Gladly," she replied, returning to her desk.

"How old was it?" Frank asked.

Starkey just kept shaking his head. "I'm under instructions from my insurance company not to say anything. I'm sure you understand."

"Were there problems before?"

"No," Starkey said. "No more questions."

The secretary popped her head in the door. "Airport security is on the way."

"They were just leaving," Starkey said.

Joe looked Starkey right in the eyes. "We're leaving," he said, "but we're going to find out what happened—with or without your help."

Joe kept careful watch in the rearview mirror as he and Frank pulled out of the airport and headed home. Apparently, Starkey had called off security once they'd left the hangar, because no one was coming after them.

As Joe pulled the van into the driveway at home, he thought maybe he'd relaxed too soon. There was a plain sedan with government plates parked across the street. "I think we have a visitor," he warned.

"I bet it's Hutchens," Frank said as they hopped out of the van. Bursting into the kitchen, the Hardys were surprised to find a tall, suntanned man rifling through their refrigerator.

"Excuse me, fellas," the man said. "Didn't expect you back so soon." He plopped a carton of orange juice onto the kitchen counter, wiped his mouth with a handkerchief, and straightened his tie. "I'm Mark Mitchell, regional supervisor of the National Transpor—"

"Right, the NTSB," Joe interrupted. "What are you doing in our kitchen?"

"Sorry. I didn't mean to alarm you. Your mother said to help myself, that you'd be home soon. She just went out to run a few errands."

"Sure," Joe said. He picked up the orange juice and put it back in the refrigerator.

"Listen," Mitchell said, running a hand through his dark hair before checking his watch. "You're Frank, right?"

"Right," Frank said.

"Well, Frank, I think Hutchens is giving you

a bad rap. He's a hard case, you know, a real tough guy."

"What specifically are you getting at?" Frank asked.

Mitchell shot his cuffs and reached into his jacket pocket. "This is the temporary suspension of your license," he said, handing Frank a neatly folded sheet of paper. "Hutchens wants to have a hearing immediately—today or tomorrow. He's taking his evidence to the Federal Aviation Administration. I want to help you, you know, make sure things go the way they should. That's why I came by myself."

"How're you going to do that?"

"I'll just slow Hutchens down a bit, you know." Mitchell checked his watch again and started for the door. He slapped Frank on the back. "Don't worry. It's only a temporary suspension. I'll get Hutchens to cool off and we'll get to the truth. I promise I'll take care of it, okay?"

"Okay, thanks," Frank said. This all seemed to be happening too quickly.

Mitchell had the door open and was about to leave, when he turned and asked one last question. "Do either of you know a James Ericson?"

Joe shrugged and looked at Frank.

"He's about your size," Mitchell said, gesturing toward Joe. "He's got real 1950s rock and roll hair, like Elvis Presley."

Joe started to mention the incident at the airport, but Frank cut him off. "Never heard of the guy. Is he important to the case?"

"Oh, it's nothing, I'm sure," Mitchell replied. He gave the Hardys a quick smile and a wink. "We have to keep our investigation confidential, you know. Just let me know if he or Hutchens tries to contact you, okay?" He was already out on the front walk, striding for his car. "And don't worry, Frank. I'll make sure Hutchens gives you a fair shake."

"Do you believe that guy?" Joe asked after Mitchell had pulled away. "He was talking to us like we were nine years old."

"He seems to be on top of things, though," Frank said. "Now we know who James Ericson is, and it sounds like he and Hutchens are up to something."

"How do you figure they're connected?"

"I don't know," Frank said. "I just hope Mitchell keeps his promise to get Hutchens off my back. In the meantime, I say we go back to Starkey tonight and take a good look at those maintenance files."

Joe spent the rest of the afternoon doing homework while his brother visited Callie at the hospital. Once they had dinner it was time to head back to the airport. They told their mom that they were going to check on Callie at the hospital and might stop for a milk shake on the way home.

* * *

Joe's flashlight illuminated a row of World War II fighter planes—a German Messerschmitt Bf 109E, a Japanese Mitsubishi A6M Zero, and an American P51-D Mustang, with its distinctive smooth sharklike nose and underbelly—in John Starkey's office.

"Look at this," Joe whispered, picking up a plastic model from the credenza behind Starkey's desk. "He's even got a Russian MiG-3. Check out the low canopy on this thing. How did the pilot even see out?"

"Joe," Frank scolded, "we've got work to do."

"Right." Joe put down the plane and started going through Starkey's desk, one drawer at a time. It had been easy picking the locks and getting in, but that didn't mean they had any time to waste.

Frank found some antique wooden file cabinets by the door and began flipping through files. Every few minutes he peered out through the outer office and into the hangar area, making sure no one surprised them. Things seemed quiet.

"I don't see much," Joe said, opening another drawer. "They've got a lot of bills to pay. That might force them to cut corners on maintenance, I guess."

"Having bills to pay isn't against the law," Frank said. He closed the cabinet. "Is that a computer over there?"

Joe shot the beam of his flashlight against the

far wall. A smaller desk sat in the corner. "Yep," he said. "Want me to check it out?"

"Finish with the desk, I'll check the computer." Frank went over and turned on the computer. He found two files on the hard drive with dates as their titles. He clicked on file "Jan.22." A long text file filled the screen. "Hey, I've got something."

Joe looked up.

"There's all kinds of information here about a crash that happened last winter."

"A Starkey plane?"

"Right, a twin-engine float plane. It looks like they rented it to some guy running ice-fishing charters up into Canada."

"What happened?"

"Hold on." Frank scrolled through more text. There were photographs that had obviously been scanned into the hard disk, and copies of reports on official NTSB letterhead. The photographs showed a plane half buried in a snowbank. One of the landing pontoons had been ripped off, and the plane had actually broken in two at the tail. It lay there, delicately cracked open like an eggshell.

"Seems that Hutchens fielded this crash, too," Frank said. "Hmmm. He ruled pilot error. They forgot to de-ice the wings."

"How about the passengers?"

"Amazing," Frank said. "They all walked away. Only a few scratches."

Joe held up his hands suddenly, calling for silence. The brothers listened for several long moments but heard nothing.

"Okay," Joe said, leaning down to check the lowest drawers of the desk. "Frank," he added, "you should get the name of the pilot in that crash. Maybe he doesn't think it was his fault."

"Good idea." Frank opened the next file. "Here's another one," he said. "June, just over four months ago." The photos on this one were pretty grim. A single-engine plane, just like the one Frank had rented, had gone down in a wooded area.

"What happened with that one?" Joe asked.

"Hold on, I'm reading." Frank scanned the details from the text, but his eyes kept going back to the photographs. The plane was stuck high in the branches of a tree like a lost kite. It hung there, a little crooked. The pilot's door was ripped off, and the seat belt dangled down. Farther down, strips of what looked like blood-stained clothing had snagged on smaller, sharper branches.

"Hutchens ruled pilot error again," Frank said quietly. "He figured they ran out of gas."

"What?" Joe didn't sound convinced.

"It's pretty common," Frank said. "People pay close attention to their navigational gauges and forget about the fuel level."

"If you say so. Did you get the name of the pilot in that one. Maybe we can call him, too."

"No go," Frank answered. "He and his passenger were both killed."

"Oh."

Frank began copying the files onto floppy disks. He wanted to read all this stuff more carefully later. Joe had found a small metal lock box in one of Starkey's desk drawers and had it up on the desktop. He concentrated on jimmying it open.

"I found the maintenance records," Frank said.

"Good going."

"The aircraft we rented was just in the shop for two weeks. We were the first people to fly her since she had been put back in service."

"That was some test drive," Joe said. "Who signed off on the work?"

"Looks like James Ericson," Frank said. "He must be a mechanic here along with Buddy Berkemeier."

"Another good reason to have a talk with 'Elvis' Ericson," Joe said.

"They've got fourteen planes," Frank noted. "And a couple of those jets are over twenty-five years old."

"They don't look it," Joe said. He finally had the steel box open, but it contained only family photographs and some trinkets from air shows around the country.

"They do look well maintained," Frank agreed, "but according to these records, most of them have been out of service at least once in the last six months."

Frank looked up just in time to see a shadow fill the office door, blocking out the light from the hangar.

The shadow suddenly took shape. It was the silhouette of a man in the doorway, holding a gun in his right hand.

Frank saw the shadow pointing the gun straight at Joe. Realizing that the man hadn't noticed him sitting off to the side at the computer, Frank let his hands glide over the surface of the desk, keeping his eyes on the figure.

"Freeze!" the shadow voice said, sounding nervous.

Joe put his hands up and started to stand.

Frank's hand found a stone paperweight. But as he raised his hand to hurl it, there was a loud bang and a flash. The concussion echoed off the hangar walls, and Frank was blinded for a split second. Then he saw Joe collapse in a heap behind the desk.

Chapter 6

JOE HADN'T NOTICED the figure in the doorway until it ordered him to freeze. He reacted instinctively, holding his hands up and starting to stand. That was when the gun went off.

Joe felt something sharp sting his face. He dropped to the floor, thinking he was hit. But he was okay. The bullet had hit the top of the desk and sent splinters flying at him. He popped back up as if he were on the football field, ready for the next play.

The shadow retreated from the doorway, and Joe went after him. He heard Frank's voice behind him say, "Joe, he's still got the gun." But he didn't care; he wasn't going to let this guy come after him like that again.

The figure darted behind a jet and stopped. Joe held up. He could see the gunman's legs. Did the guy think he was hiding? Maybe he was just waiting for Joe to come around the nose of the plane so he could plug him at close range.

Joe sprinted toward the jet. At the last second he dove like a baseball player sliding headfirst into second base. He skidded under the plane, smashing his head into the gunman's shins.

The blow whipped the man's feet out from under him and slammed him to the cement floor. Joe was on the guy like a wild animal, grabbing his gun hand by the wrist and pummeling him with two quick shots to the face.

Frank came up just as Joe wrenched the pistol from the man's hand and stood up over him.

"Nice slide," Frank said. "Way to break up the double play."

"Look who we have here," Joe said, catching his breath. "John Starkey."

Starkey held his hand to his bleeding mouth. "What do you expect?" he said angrily. "This is my place. You were trespassing and going through my things. I was within my rights to protect my property from thieves." His speech wore down and ground to a halt.

"Come on, get up." Frank helped Starkey to his feet. "Let's go back to your office and talk. I think we all have a lot to say."

Back in the office, Joe turned on the light while

Frank helped Starkey to sit down at his desk. He seemed shaken but okay.

"What are you doing here?" he finally asked.

Joe sat down on the edge of the desk and examined Starkey's gun, an old Smith & Wesson .357 Magnum. "I was trying to get the answers you wouldn't give us this morning, when you decided to shoot me."

Starkey ran his fingers over the small trench the slug had made in the top of his desk. "I-I didn't mean to fire the gun," he stammered. "I was just nervous."

"What do you have to be nervous about?" Frank asked. "Who did you think we were?"

"I didn't notice *you* at all," Starkey replied. "I only saw your brother here and thought James had come back." Starkey looked at Joe sheepishly. "You moved and I accidentally pulled the trigger."

"You thought I was James Ericson?" Joe asked.

"That's right."

"Who is this guy Ericson?"

"He's Brenda's boyfriend," Starkey said. He wiped his forehead with the back of his hand. "He's been working for me as a mechanic for almost a year."

"What was that big argument about this morning?" Frank said.

"I fired the punk," Starkey said.

"Hold on," Joe said. "Let's start at the beginning. Why'd you fire him?"

Starkey took a deep breath. "A couple of months after James started working for me, we had our first crash," he began.

"The fishing charter?" Frank asked.

"Right," Starkey said. "Fifteen years I ran this business with no problems—not a single thing went wrong. Then two months after I hire Ericson, one of our planes goes down."

"But Hutchens ruled pilot error," Joe said. "What does that have to do with Ericson?"

"Hutchens *finally* ruled pilot error," Starkey said. "He investigated that accident for weeks. He kept looking for something wrong with the plane, but he couldn't find anything. No, he couldn't find anything wrong even though he tried for a long time."

"Then there was another accident, wasn't there?" Frank said.

Starkey bowed his head. "Yes," he said slowly. "There was another crash."

"And two people died," Joe said.

"That's right. Two dead."

"But Hutchens ruled pilot error again."

"He went over the aircraft with a fine-tooth comb; it took him almost three weeks. And he finally decided they ran out of gas."

"Do you believe it?" Frank asked.

Starkey buried his face in his hands. "I don't

know what to believe," he said. "I just don't know anymore."

"All right, calm down," Joe said, standing up to put his hand on the older man's shoulder.

Frank got Starkey a cup of water from the water cooler. "You think Ericson had something to do with it?"

"Like I told you, I don't know. All I know is that right after he begins working here planes start dropping out of the sky." Starkey took a sip of water. "Then two weeks ago Bryan Hutchens comes to me and says he has evidence that I'm using black-market plane parts and doctoring maintenance records."

"Is that true? You've obviously sunk a lot of money into this place," Frank said. "Are you having cash-flow problems?"

"It's tough to run a business these days," Starkey said. "But I'd never do anything to endanger our customers. Never."

"So you're sure your parts are okay?" Joe asked, leaning in close to Starkey.

Starkey hesitated. "Well, I run the business. But I don't pay as close attention to all the paperwork as I used to. I'm trying to get out of the office and drum up business, you know."

"So . . ."

"So after Hutchens came by I went over the maintenance records. I found out that James had switched parts suppliers without my knowledge."

"I thought Buddy was the chief mechanic," Frank said.

Starkey smiled. "Buddy's been with me since the beginning," he said. "He's a great mechanic, the best. He's never even asked me for a raise the whole time he's been here. How about that?"

Frank nodded, trying to act impressed.

"Buddy's not big on paperwork and phone calls, though," Starkey continued. "I'm sure he wasn't even aware of what James was doing."

"What did you say to Ericson?" Joe asked.

"I confronted him with it. He said he didn't know what I was talking about. He claimed he never filled out a parts order, claimed he had no idea what Hutchens was up to."

"So you fired him?"

"And told him to stay away from my daughter," Starkey said. "What a loser, coming around here to see her even after I canned him . . ."

Frank went over to the computer desk and when Starkey wasn't watching put the disks he'd copied into his shirt pocket. "Have you talked to Hutchens recently?"

"Sure, yesterday he told me that he's already started the paperwork to get the FAA to revoke my charter license," Starkey replied. "This third accident is going to close us up for good."

Joe stood up and emptied the shells from Starkey's gun. He then tossed it back to the man. "I think we should go pay Hutchens a visit," he said to his brother.

"Sounds good."

Starkey fumbled the gun, and it fell to the floor. "No," he said. "No, I don't think we should do that. It's late."

"The sooner we find out what's going on the better," Frank said. "Hutchens is trying to cancel my license, too."

Starkey stood up. "Okay, fine," he said, but Frank could tell the man was terrified.

The three of them left the hangar and walked across the field toward the parking lot. The Hardys flanked Starkey. The boys had to keep stopping to let him catch up. He kept lagging behind, first to tie his shoe, next to make sure he had his keys.

They got into the van, Frank climbing in back while Joe shut Starkey into the passenger seat and walked around to the driver's side. Then, as they were pulling out of their parking place, Starkey bolted. He yanked open his door and leaped out, rolling on the pavement.

Frank slid open the side door, but when Joe slammed on the brakes the door rocketed shut along its tracks. Frank pulled his hand back just in time.

"Stay inside," Joe yelled. "He's already made it to his car. I'll cut him off."

The engine stalled when Joe popped the van

into gear. He had to restart the car before stomping on the accelerator and taking off. They saw the headlights of Starkey's sedan bouncing up and down in the darkness as he four-wheeled his way over parking dividers and curbs to get out to the access road.

The Hardys followed, keeping Starkey in their sights as they bounded over a grassy median between two sections of the parking lot.

"We're gaining on him," Frank yelled.

Joe braced himself as the van bucked over a final curb and rebounded like a bronco. They were right on Starkey's tail when both vehicles reached the highway. Pulling up until the bumper of the van was touching Starkey's trunk, Joe blasted his horn and flipped on his brights.

Starkey swerved to the side, dangerously near the guardrail.

"Watch it," Frank said. "We don't want to cause an accident."

Joe started to pull around the sedan but saw lights in the distance that made him hesitate.

"What is it?" Frank asked.

Joe squinted ahead. "I don't know."

The two speeding cars crested the hill and at once the night horizon was full of flashing red and blue lights.

"It's the cops," Joe said as two police cars, light bars flashing, appeared out of the distance.

The cruisers stopped, one in each lane, and blocked the highway.

Joe hit the brakes hard. Ahead of them, Starkey swerved. His car fishtailed once to the right, then snapped back around and spun out all the way. He came to a stop just a few feet from the police cars.

Joe killed the engine, and the two brothers got out and rushed to the scene.

"Stay back," one of the officers said, stepping out of the darkness to block the Hardys' path. The other officer pulled Starkey from his car.

Frank and Joe watched as the second officer, whom they quickly recognized as Con Riley, their friend on the force, placed handcuffs on Starkey and started reading him his rights: "John Starkey, you are under arrest for the murder of Bryan Hutchens. You have the right to remain silent. You have the right to counsel . . ."

Chapter 7

Frank sat down in one of the hard, straight-backed chairs in the lobby of the Bayport police department while Joe went to the vending machine to get himself a candy bar. The desk sergeant gave Frank a look of exasperation.

"Why don't you two go home to bed?" he said to Frank. "There's nothing for you here."

"We're just waiting for Officer Riley," Frank replied. Riley was the one cop in the department willing to keep them informed. Since he'd been the one to arrest Starkey, Frank figured he'd be out shortly and could fill them in on the details.

"You'll just be in the way here. Go on home."

But the Hardys stayed put. A few minutes later Riley came in, greeting the sergeant with a sober nod. He led the Hardys to an empty interrogation room, closed the door behind them, and tossed a sealed plastic bag on the wooden table. It landed with a clank of metal. "Well," he said, taking a chair and straddling it, his arms resting across the backrest. "Looks like an open-and-shut case to me.

"Bryan Hutchens was beaten to death," Riley continued. "It looks like someone pistol-whipped him. We've got a witness who saw Starkey leaving the scene, and we've got a bloody footprint in Hutchens's office that looks to be a pretty good match for Starkey's right shoe."

"Any blood in his car?" Frank asked.

Riley nodded. "All over the driver's side floorboards."

"And you've also got these," Frank said, picking up the plastic bag.

"We haven't figured out what they are yet," Riley said. "We found them in Starkey's car."

Frank knew what they were—the missing engine mounts from the wreckage—but he kept quiet. "What does your witness say?"

"It's Mark Mitchell," Riley said, "Hutchens's supervisor. He found the body and called us. He also found a copy of a letter from Hutchens to the FAA, sent earlier today. He was contacting the FAA about canceling Starkey's business license."

"So we heard," Joe said.

"What does Starkey say?" Frank asked.

"He pretty much clammed up," Riley said. "But this is the way we figure it. Hutchens tells Starkey he's out of business; Starkey goes over to talk about it—maybe he figures the gun will make what he has to say more persuasive, but he doesn't plan to shoot the guy. Once he gets there, though, Hutchens won't play ball, they have a fight, Starkey nails Hutchens over the head with the gun. That's it. Case closed."

"You'll find Starkey's gun in his office," Joe said. "It's an S and W three-fifty-seven."

"Thanks," Riley said. "I've already got someone on the way out there. Once we find traces of Hutchens's blood on the handle of the gun, Starkey's going away for a long time."

The Hardys thanked Riley for the information, went outside to the van, and headed home. It was late. "I guess you had a reason not to tell Con that those were our missing engine mounts," Joe said on the way.

"I figured Con may have the answer to how Hutchens died," Frank said, "but we still have all the same questions about what happened to our airplane. For instance, is Starkey trying to cover up faulty maintenance?"

"That would explain the mounts being in his car," Joe said. "But why didn't I find that letter Hutchens wrote to the FAA when I searched his office?"

"You searched his office yesterday, so maybe he wrote it today," Frank answered. "What I'm wondering is why Hutchens was about to shut Starkey down for not maintaining his aircraft, if he kept ruling pilot error?"

"Maybe he knew Starkey was cutting corners and the old man was paying him off to keep quiet about it," Joe speculated. "That would explain Starkey's money problems. And when Starkey wouldn't go along with their arrangement anymore, Hutchens came up with the letter."

"It's possible," Frank said. "The only sure thing is that we've got a lot more investigating to do."

"And I need some sleep," Joe said. He couldn't wait to flop down on his bed and forget about everything for a few hours.

Phil Cohen stopped by early the next day, Saturday, carrying a sheaf of papers. "I've got the results from the machine shop analysis," he said, making himself comfortable at the breakfast table.

Joe flipped through the charts and numbers while munching on a piece of bacon. "What's all this gibberish mean?"

"It means," Frank said, looking over his shoulder, "that the parts we took off the plane aren't up to FAA standards."

"But that's not all," Phil said. He jumped up

and pointed to three columns of numbers. "These are the heat and stress tests they did on the mounts. Notice the difference?"

Frank nodded slowly. "Why is that?"

"We found one shiny new mount, remember? It didn't have any grease on it."

"What about it?"

"It's perfect," Phil said. "All the other pieces I had analyzed suffered from metal fatigue, even the struts we pulled from the landing gear. They were basically made of pot metal, the left-over scrap after you purify iron and aluminum."

"Total trash," Joe said.

"Exactly, except for that one mount. It was right up to spec. Which means—"

"Which means," Frank said, "that the person we chased out of the hangar was replacing the bad parts with good ones so that it would look like pilot error."

Phil signaled thumbs-up. "Which also means that person knew which parts were likely to fail and how to replace them."

"James Ericson," Joe said.

"Or John Starkey," Frank added. "We know Starkey might use bogus parts to save money, but we still don't have a motive for Ericson. Why would he put bad parts in Starkey's planes?"

"Oh, come on, Frank," Joe said. "This kind of thing happens all the time." He dropped the charts on the table and went to the skillet for more bacon. "Ericson's a con man. He got close to Brenda so her father would hire him. Then he orders faulty parts and gets cash kickbacks from whoever manufactures them. Remember, Ericson's name was on the parts orders."

"Right," Phil said. "And it was Ericson Joe saw at the hangar that night, not Starkey."

"But how did Hutchens fit in?" Frank sat down. "Obviously, someone was switching the parts to screw up the investigation. Was Hutchens totally innocent? Was he ruling pilot error because someone fixed the planes before he got to them, or . . ."

"Or was he in on it with Ericson?" Joe said.

Frank made a face at his brother.

"Okay, okay," Joe said. "Or he was in on it with Ericson and Starkey? Does that make you happy? The point is, Hutchens could have helped Ericson cover his tracks so they could keep saying it was pilot error and keep extorting money from Starkey. Or they could all be in on it together so Starkey could save money on parts. Whatever. I just don't think Hutchens was innocent, Frank. Remember, he was in a pretty big hurry to say our crash was all your fault."

Frank sat at the table and tapped the tines of his fork against his plate. "We need to find out where those parts came from," he said finally. "Follow me."

Up in his room, Frank loaded one of the disks

he'd found in Starkey's office into his computer. "Here it is," he said. "Right after Ericson started working for Starkey, they changed parts suppliers."

"Pickell Machine Works," Joe read aloud. "Out of Baton Rouge, Louisiana."

Frank picked up the phone. "I'm going to call Pickell and see what they have to say." He dialed the number.

Phil and Joe watched Frank patiently holding the receiver to his ear for almost a minute. Finally he punched in some numbers and hung up.

"What was that all about?" Joe asked.

"It was strange," Frank said. "No one answered. A machine asked me to punch in my number."

"It's a paging system," Phil said. "They'll call you back."

"Maybe," Joe said.

"That would make sense," Frank said. "If you were making fake airplane parts, you wouldn't want anyone to track you down too easily. I bet the address on these invoices is fake."

Joe nodded just as the phone rang.

Frank picked up and put the other person on the speaker. "Hello," he said.

"Who's calling?" a raspy voice demanded.

"My name's Frank. I got your number from a friend of mine here in Bayport. I hear you have a special discount program, and I'm interested."

There was a pause and the sound of papers

shuffling. "We aren't taking any more orders right now," the voice said.

Frank leaned forward to say something into the speaker, but the line went dead.

"Something spooked him," Phil said.

Frank hung up and turned off the computer.

"I say we go down there," Joe said. "The Bayport PD's on top of things here, and if Mitchell catches us doing our own investigation he might never give you your license back."

Frank looked doubtful.

"Just a quick trip," Joe said. "The parts are the only trail lead we have."

"But who knows where it leads," Frank said. "Okay, we go." He looked at Phil. "We need your help. Can you stay here and keep an eye on Brenda Starkey? I bet Ericson won't be too far away from wherever she is, and Mitchell won't recognize you if you cross paths."

Phil nodded. "You got it."

An hour later, after packing and leaving a note for their mom, Frank and Joe arrived at the airport. They had a deal with their dad that they could charge plane flights if necessary and his PI business would pick up the tab—provided the trips were crucial to solving a case. If not, they'd end up mowing a lot of lawns to pay for the flights themselves. They had just booked their flight when Frank spotted Mark Mitchell striding across the field toward a private plane.

"I'll be right back," Frank said to Joe. He flashed his ticket, hurried through security, and caught up with Mitchell just as he was about to climb the steps into his plane.

"Inspector Mitchell, how's it going?" Frank asked.

"Things have been better," Mitchell replied, checking his watch. "I'm in kind of a hurry. Can we talk when I get back?"

"I was just wondering if there was any news on my case."

"I'm investigating all of Hutchens's cases," Mitchell said. "The thing with Starkey may have just been the tip of the iceberg." Mitchell held out his hand to shake. "Frank, I promise we'll get all this straightened out, okay? Talk to you soon." Then he climbed the steps two at a time and disappeared into the plane.

Jetting all over as a regional NTSB inspector must be a cool job, Frank thought as he headed back inside the terminal. He was surprised to see Brenda Starkey standing next to Joe, her hands on her hips.

"I'm going with you," she said curtly.

"You told her where we were going?"

Joe frowned. "She sneaked up behind me and looked at my ticket."

"You're not going with us," Frank said.

"Oh, yes, I am."

"No way," Joe said. As Ericson's girlfriend, Brenda was right at the top of his suspect list. He wouldn't be surprised if she'd turned on her father. People had done stranger things for love.

"You don't have a choice," Brenda said.

"No," Joe said. "*You* don't."

"You heard what happened to Hutchens?" Brenda asked, moving her face close to Joe's ear.

"Sure," Joe answered.

"Well," she whispered, her eyes narrowing, "if I don't go with you, your little friend Phil is going to be next."

Chapter 8

JOE MET BRENDA'S GAZE. "What's that supposed to mean?"

Brenda arched an eyebrow at Joe. "Just don't make a big commotion, or Phil gets it," she said.

"Where is he?" Frank asked.

Brenda led the Hardys away from the ticket counter. "He's fine, for now," she said. "James and I spotted him following us, and now we have him in a nice, secluded place. If I don't go with you, James is going to inflict a little pain on him. So it's up to you—yes or no?"

Joe was seething. "Phil has nothing to do with this," he said. "Let him go."

"Hold on, Joe," Frank said. He took his brother by the arm and quickly led him away from Brenda.

"Hey, where are you going?" Brenda asked, sounding a bit nervous.

"We'll be right back."

When they were out of earshot, Frank said, "Give me the cell phone." Joe pulled it out of his carry-on bag and handed it to Frank, who flipped it open and punched in a number.

"Phil," he said, "it's Frank. Where are you?"

Joe leaned in close so he could hear. Phil's voice crackled over the phone. "Hey, Frank. I'm sorry, buddy. I found Brenda visiting her father in jail and started tracking her, but she spotted me when she stopped for gas."

"You're okay, then?" Frank asked. "You aren't with Ericson?"

"No way," Phil answered. "I'm sitting by myself at Mr. Pizza, just about to dig into a double pepperoni pie."

"You didn't see Ericson at all?"

Phil sounded apologetic. "No, Frank, sorry. And I might have let it slip to Brenda that you were headed to Baton Rouge. Did she come after you guys at the airport?"

"Yep. What happened, Phil?"

"Oh, man. She came up to my car and started screaming at me. All these people at the gas station must've thought I was some kind of crazy stalker or something the way she was coming down on me. She was going on about me following her and how her father and Ericson are both innocent and blah, blah, blah. I just lost it and told her you were going to Baton Rouge to prove Ericson was guilty. I'm really sorry, Frank."

"It's okay, Phil. We'll be in touch." Frank shut down the phone and smiled at Joe. "She's bluffing."

They marched back over to Brenda.

"You aren't going anywhere," Joe said. "Because we just talked to Phil, and he's enjoying a nice early lunch all by himself."

Brenda's face went white, then started to turn red. "Okay, so I was bluffing," she said quickly. "But that should prove something to you."

"What would that be?" Joe said.

"I caught Phil following me. James and I could easily have turned the tables on him and held him hostage if we wanted to. But we didn't."

"So?" Frank asked.

"So as I've been trying to tell you all along," Brenda said, "my father and James are innocent. They'd never intentionally hurt anybody."

"Right," Joe said. "James's beaning me on the head with a lead pipe was just his way of saying 'hello.' "

"He didn't know who you were then," Brenda said. "He thought you were with whoever was messing with the plane that night."

"What about Ericson's name on all the parts orders?" Joe asked.

Brenda shook her head. "He doesn't order the

parts, Buddy does. James just fills out the paperwork to help me out. If it was up to Buddy, it would never get done."

Joe turned to his brother. "Do you believe this?" he whispered. "Now she's trying to frame Buddy. She'll do anything to cover for her man Elvis."

"So you're saying we're on the same team," Frank said to Brenda. "We're all interested in discovering the truth about our accident."

"And who killed Hutchens," Brenda said. "Because it wasn't my father."

"Okay," Frank said. "Here's the deal. Promise to get us in to Pickell Machine Works and you can go with us."

"Frank, that's nuts," Joe muttered.

"Deal," Brenda said.

As Brenda went to a phone booth to make a call to Pickell, Joe berated his brother. "What were you thinking?" he asked. "She's in on it with all of them."

"Maybe," Frank conceded. "But at least this way we'll be able to keep an eye on her, and it makes getting inside Pickell just about automatic."

Joe shrugged. "All right, but we're really going to have to watch it."

"Don't we always?" Frank said.

Brenda returned. "It's all set," she said. "I told them I'm bringing two friends down to Baton

Rouge who want to start an aviation firm. They'll be happy to meet with you."

Joe got the last laugh when they boarded the jet for Louisiana. He and Frank sat together comfortably, but since Brenda had purchased her ticket separately, she had to sit farther back, next to a stranger.

"Poor Brenda," Joe said sarcastically. "Looks like she's next to a talker."

Frank looked back a few rows. Brenda was wedged into the window seat next to a really strange-looking man who was talking nonstop.

Brenda gave Frank a pained expression and waved. Frank smiled and waved back. "The guy looks like a werewolf," he said to Joe.

He had wild, bushy eyebrows, sideburns, and yellow-blond hair like a lion's. "Nice sunglasses," Joe said. "I wouldn't want to run into that guy in a dark alley."

"Brenda's in for a fun trip."

Four hours later the three of them landed in Baton Rouge, Louisiana's capital and the second largest city after New Orleans.

"So," Joe said, "someone's going to meet us at the airport hotel, is that the plan?"

Frank closed the magazine he was reading. "That's what Brenda said. Just check in and wait for them to call."

"Waiting," Joe groaned. "My favorite game."

Inside, the terminal was comfortably air-conditioned, but Frank could see heat ghosts rising off the field outside. "I bet it's about ninety-five degrees out there," he said.

"I'm just glad to get off the plane," Brenda said. "I thought that guy was going to talk me to death."

"I figured you'd have a date by now," Joe said.

"Yeah, sure. The man of my dreams."

They took a shuttle bus over to the airport hotel, checked in, and settled down to wait for the call from Pickell. Joe found a football game on TV while Frank pored over the latest issue of *Aviation* magazine.

About an hour later Brenda came over from her room. "I just got the call," she said. "They want to meet us downstairs in five minutes."

Joe clicked off the television. "I'm ready."

"No, you're not," Frank said, throwing Joe a tie. "Put this on. We're supposed to look like businessmen."

Joe muttered something, but put his tie on anyway.

Two men approached them as soon as they stepped off the elevator in the lobby.

"Miss Starkey?" A wiry, middle-aged man with dry, wrinkled skin transferred a cigarette to his left hand and held out his right. "I'm Bob

Pickell," he said. "The president. And this is Jerry Cook, quality control supervisor."

"Pleased to meet you—finally," Brenda said.

"Likewise."

Frank noticed that Cook held back a little. He was about medium height and balding. His body was soft and undefined, as if he hadn't exercised a day in his life, and he had dark, deep-set eyes.

After the introductions, Pickell motioned for them to follow him. "Our car is out front," he said, taking a drag off his cigarette, then immediately going into a coughing fit.

Pickell Machine Works turned out to be only minutes away. It was a boxy, prefabricated steel building on the edge of the airport. It had few windows and no signs, but it did have its own taxiway to one of the shorter runways.

As Pickell and Cook gave them a tour of the plant, Frank and Brenda spun out the thread of their story.

"Frank and Joe are starting a commuter service to Philadelphia," Brenda said.

"Philadelphia and Washington, D.C.," Frank added. "If you want to get to Philly or D.C., you have to take the train or make a connection in New York," he continued. "I think we can provide a service Bayport needs."

"Sounds like you have it all worked out," Cook said evenly.

"Yes, sir," Joe said. "We're buying second-hand planes, though. We'll be needing someone to provide parts—reasonably priced, if you know what I mean."

Cook didn't respond, but Pickell grinned and patted Joe on the shoulder. "We know exactly what you mean, son."

They entered a room filled with several boxcar-size machine tool fabricators. Pickell let his cigarette dangle from his mouth as he placed a hunk of pure aluminum in a clamp at one end of a fabricator. "Watch this," he said.

He punched in some codes on a panel and the machine went to work, grinding away at the aluminum block. Less than thirty seconds later, it popped out at the other end.

"Look at that," Frank said.

The alloy square was now a precisely turned intake valve for an aircraft engine. It glinted in the light like a piece of lost treasure.

Pickell coughed a few times, then picked up the valve and handed it to Frank. "It's yours to keep," he said, the cigarette bobbing up and down in the corner of his mouth as he spoke.

Frank acted impressed. "I bet you can turn out hundreds of these in a very short period of time."

"You bet."

"We might need that many in a few years," Joe said grandly. "We've got a ten-year plan to branch out and become a major player in the air freight market. If you treat us right, we'll keep doing business with Pickell Machine Works when we hit the big time."

"Don't you worry, son," Bob Pickell said. "I think this partnership could be very profitable for all of us." He held out his hand to shake. "I've got an idea," he said. "How about we talk turkey tonight. The entertainment's on me. How's that sound?"

"Sounds great," Frank replied. He noticed that Cook didn't seem overly thrilled.

Pickell lit another cigarette. "We'll be spending the evening on the *Proud Mary*—that's one of Baton Rouge's casino boats. We'll have a grand old time."

"You're a good man to do business with," Joe said. He decided this was his chance to snoop around. "Is there a washroom where I can freshen up before we go?" he asked.

"Sure. Up the stairs and to the right."

Joe figured he had ten minutes at most to get a look around. He jogged up the stairs two at a time, coming to a hallway leading off in both directions. Spying the bathroom to his right, he turned down the opposite hall, discovering a row of offices.

He couldn't see anything to indicate which office belonged to whom until he found one at the end of the hall that had an ashtray heaped with stubbed-out cigarette butts. Quietly, he closed the door behind him.

Pickell's desk was as messy as Hutchens's had been clean. How could he find anything in this mess? He was about to throw up his hands in frustration when a crisp, clean manila folder jumped into view. It sat right on top of the biggest pile of papers.

Joe opened it. Bingo. Letters printed on NTSB letterhead tumbled out of the folder. Gathering them together, Joe noticed they had Hutchens's signature on the bottom. He didn't have time to read them; he'd just copy them and they could check them over later. He went over to an old desktop copier and flipped the switch. A light came on saying, "Please wait—copier warming up."

"Come on, come on," Joe said. He glanced at the door. Soon they'd start wondering where he was. Finally the Ready light came on and Joe loaded the first letter. The machine slowly scanned the page, making a loud groaning sound. "Shhh," he told it. "Be quiet."

The copier went silent, and the green Ready light came on again. Joe heard a click behind him—the door.

As he started to turn he felt a powerful hand clamp down on the back of his neck. A deep voice said, "Need help finding something?"

Chapter 9

INSTINCTIVELY JOE DROPPED his chin to his chest, protecting his throat. He thrust his elbow behind him, but it missed because his attacker had neatly sidestepped the blow.

"Whoa there," the man said as Joe whirled to face him. "I don't want to fight, man."

It was the shaggy-haired guy who'd been sitting next to Brenda on the airplane. "Who are you?" Joe demanded. "Did you follow us off the plane?"

"It doesn't matter who I am," the stranger said. "We're on the same team."

Joe couldn't read the expression behind the surfer-style, wraparound shades.

"We don't have much time," the guy said. "Let

me see what you've got." He held out his hand for the folder.

"No way," Joe replied. "First you tell me who you are and what's going on."

Without saying anything, the man tried to grab the file from Joe, but Joe was done asking questions. He balled up his fist and threw a left hook right into the guy's gut.

"*Ooommph.*" The air rushed from the man's lungs and he doubled over, bracing himself against Pickell's desk.

Joe grabbed the guy by the hair to straighten him up. "You're going to tell me who—what?"

As he pulled, the man's hair started to come off in Joe's hand and he found himself holding nothing but a fuzzy blond wig. Joe tossed the disguise aside and put a hammerlock on the guy's head, standing him up and almost lifting him off the floor.

"Ericson." Joe held tight, his right arm around the mechanic's neck like a vise. "I owe you one," he said. With his left hand he peeled away the fake sideburns and eyebrows. They made the sound of bandages being ripped off, and Ericson winced.

"So you're trying to cover your tracks, aren't you?" Joe asked. "Too bad for you I've got the evidence here that's going to put you away."

Ericson tried to talk, but Joe's chokehold cut off his air. Joe loosened his grip. Ericson coughed and gasped. "I swear," he whispered hoarsely. "I swear I had nothing to do with it. Somebody's framing me. Me and Brenda's dad."

Joe tightened up on the mechanic's throat. "Sure," he said. "You're as innocent as a little lamb." He had to figure out what to do with Ericson while he finished copying the file. Pickell and Cook would probably be upstairs looking for him any minute. He glanced around the room, spotting a closet with what looked like a sturdy, lockable door. He started to drag Ericson toward it.

"Hey, what're you doing?" Ericson said, struggling to twist free.

Joe was reaching out to open the closet door when he heard a sharp click and the lights went out. He whirled in the direction of the hallway and instantly knew he'd made a mistake because he'd given Ericson an opening.

Joe felt himself being lifted off the ground. Then he was upside-down in midair, with barely time to brace for the impact. He landed flat on his back, unhurt but angry for letting Ericson flip him.

He bounced up, ready to give Ericson his payback. Reaching the doorway, he flipped the lights back on. It was Brenda. She stood in the door frame, chin out, hands on her hips, blocking his path. Ericson had disappeared—evidently bolting down the hall.

"Out of my way," Joe said.

"What's all the noise up here?" It was Bob Pickell, appearing behind Brenda. "I told you the bathroom was the other way," he said to Joe. "How'd you end up in my office?"

"He just tried to get fresh with me," Brenda said. "I had to teach him some manners."

Joe stared at Brenda; for once he couldn't think of what to say.

Pickell's hearty laugh quickly degenerated into a hacking cough. "Oh, my goodness," he said, catching his breath. "I certainly hope you learned your lesson, son." He clapped Joe on the back and led him back down the hall. "It's a bad idea to mix business with pleasure. Except tonight, of course," he said, winking.

Joe kept his cool, laughing along with the old man while Brenda smirked at him.

Downstairs, Frank and Cook stood by the front door. "Ready to go?" he asked when the other three returned.

"Sorry, but I'm going to have to bow out," Brenda said politely. "I've got a headache." She nodded at the Hardys. "You two go and have a good time, though."

"If you aren't going, then maybe we shouldn't go either," Frank said.

Brenda turned to Pickell. "Would you excuse us for a moment?"

Pickell lit another cigarette. "Sure, honey."

Once they were out of earshot, Joe turned to

Brenda. "What was that all about?" he hissed. He was struggling to keep his voice down.

"You should thank me," Brenda said. "I saved your skin up there."

"You saved your boyfriend, that's it."

Frank motioned for Joe to quiet down. "What's going on?"

"I found something," Joe replied. "But Ericson interrupted me. He was the guy on the plane with her, dressed up in that ridiculous disguise. I would've had the evidence now if those two hadn't tag-teamed me."

"You're just embarrassed because you lost another fight with James," Brenda taunted.

Joe started to yell at her, but Frank came between them. "I thought we were working together on this," he said.

"We are," Brenda replied. "As I said, if I hadn't shown up, Pickell would've caught Joe red-handed in his office."

"I'm keeping an eye on you," Joe said.

"No, you're not. If you and Frank don't go to the riverboat, I'll tell Pickell who you really are and why you're here."

"You can't do that."

"Watch me."

Brenda looked as if she was about to shout something to Pickell when Frank held up his hands. "Okay," he said. "We'll go."

"But, Frank . . ."

"We don't have a choice, Joe. Come on, let's go."

The Mississippi River was only a fifteen-minute drive from the airport. Moored at the city flood wall, the *Proud Mary* was a full-size replica of a nineteenth-century paddle-wheel steamer.

"Pretty impressive," Joe said as they pulled into the parking lot. "She must be two hundred fifty feet long."

The boat was four grand stories of staterooms, restaurants, and gambling parlors on a flat, bargelike deck. Two smokestacks at least twelve feet in diameter rose up into the night sky, and rows of twinkling lights draped the ship like holiday ornaments.

"That stern wheel looks big enough to power a small city," Frank said. "Does she sail or just float?"

"Oh, she goes all right," Pickell said as they climbed the boarding plank at the bow. He glanced at his watch. "She sails in ten minutes. We head down the river for an hour or so then come back and pick up more passengers."

"For the midnight cruise they always pack them in like sardines," Jerry Cook said. Frank sensed that he was uncomfortable in this gaudy environment.

A huge guy wearing a tuxedo was checking IDs at the door, but he waved the Hardys' party through, not even checking that the boys were too young to be on board. Pickell knew everyone on board.

Inside, Joe had plenty to take his mind off his scrap with Brenda. A beautiful young woman stood at every game table, dealing cards or spinning roulette wheels. They all wore short black skirts and long-sleeved, white silk blouses—the house uniform. More large men in black tuxedos stood at strategic spots in the background, hands folded in front of them, keeping a close eye on things.

"I'm in heaven," Joe said.

"So am I, boy." Pickell chuckled. "So am I." He made a beeline for the cashier's window, coming back in no time with a handful of chips. "Let's hit the tables, fellows," he said, smiling.

Frank, Joe, and Jerry followed Pickell to a blackjack table. A young woman with ringlets of golden bronze hair cascading over her shoulders greeted them with an impossibly bright and sincere smile.

Only Pickell sat down. "Come on, fellows," he said, striking a match. "We've got some celebrating to do."

"You know I don't gamble, sir," Cook said, with a tight smile.

"Oh, I wasn't talking to you. Joe, Frank, sit down here next to me."

Frank held up a hand. "I'll just watch," Frank

said, not wanting to admit he was too young to gamble.

Though Cook seemed reluctant to leave Pickell alone, Joe managed to convince him to go get something to eat.

Meanwhile, Frank stayed and watched Pickell lose just about every hand to the attractive dealer. At more than twenty-five dollars per hand, it was adding up quickly.

"I thought you'd bring good luck," Pickell said. He had the seven of hearts showing and called for another card. The dealer pulled a card from the shoe and flipped it onto Pickell's seven. The six of clubs.

"Dealer stays," the young woman said. She had a ten showing.

Pickell flipped over his hole card—the six of hearts. "Nineteen," he said.

The dealer showed her other card. Another ten.

Pickell tossed his cards down in disgust. "Twenty," he rasped, breaking into another coughing fit.

Twenty minutes later Joe and Jerry returned from the restaurant to find Pickell still losing.

Frank signaled Joe that it was time to leave. "The boat's about to dock and Joe and I have an early flight out tomorrow. We have to call it a night."

"Thanks," Joe said, shaking Pickell's hand. "It

looks like we'll be doing a lot of business together."

"You fellows are great!" Pickell exclaimed. "Sure you don't want to stick around awhile? My luck's about to change. I can feel it."

"No, thanks. But we'll be in touch."

As the Hardys headed for the exit, they overheard Cook trying to urge Pickell away from the blackjack table. He was having no luck.

Out on the wharf, the two brothers caught a cab. Instead of the airport hotel, Frank asked the driver to take them on to Pickell Machine Works.

"Pickell definitely has a gambling problem," Frank said, watching out the window as more passengers boarded the casino boat. "He must have lost over five hundred bucks."

"Cook seems concerned about him," Joe agreed. "I couldn't get any information out of the guy, though. He's a tough nut to crack."

"Maybe that file you found will give us some evidence."

"I just hope it's still there," Joe said. "If I was a gambling man, I'd bet our friends Brenda and James took this opportunity to get rid of any evidence against them."

"We'll know soon enough."

It was a dark night, with clouds shrouding the moon. After the cab left, Joe went to work on a heavy steel side door with his picks. He was having trouble getting the lock to pop, when he heard Frank's voice.

"Joe, over here. I found an open window."

Frank had pried open a window casement about eighteen inches. With a little trouble, the brothers squeezed through the opening and dropped to the floor below.

"I'll go up to Pickell's office," Joe said, shining his penlight up the stairs.

"Good," Frank replied. "I'm going to the factory floor to grab some parts. We need hard evidence that they're making counterfeits here."

The production line was an enormous warehouse of parts and machine tools barely lit by a single safety light in the far corner. At the far end of the room were the gas-fired furnaces that heated metal into a glowing, molten liquid. Beside the furnaces were standing pools of water to cool the parts when they came out of the molds.

Frank spotted big bins, the size of laundry carts, stacked high on a catwalk that reached to the thirty-foot ceiling. Computer-coded labels on each bin identified the parts by aircraft manufacturer, model year, and part number. He climbed a set of stairs to the catwalk that ran along the perimeter of the room. Finding the name of the manufacturer of the plane he rented from Starkey, Frank shined the flashlight up that row of bins, looking for engine mounts.

He was reaching into a bin when he felt something slam into the backs of his knees. He tried to stay upright, but his legs folded under him like twigs. The next thing he knew, he was staring down through the mesh grating of the catwalk at the cement floor twenty feet below. His legs burned with pain.

"Hey," he yelled. "That's enough."

He tried to get up, but his attacker slammed his head down into the grating. Frank heard the crack of his own forehead hitting steel and felt a warm trickle of blood running into his eyes.

Then he was moving, being dragged along the catwalk by his shirt collar. He grabbed for the railing but missed. He could hear the big man's heavy breathing.

Finally the thug let go. Frank scrambled to regain his footing, but there was nothing under his feet. He started to slide. Realizing he was on some kind of ramp, he shot his hands up over his head. With his fingertips, he managed to grab the lip where the ramp attached to the catwalk.

Frank turned his head and looked down behind him. The ramp led straight down into a huge vat of dark, churning liquid. A sign said Danger: Dissolving Solvent.

He scrambled to pull himself to safety, but then the man loomed over him once again. Frank tried to get a glimpse of his attacker, but the man had hoisted a bin of parts from the shelf, blocking his face. Then all at once he dumped the contents onto the ramp.

A hailstorm of nuts and bolts rained down on Frank. There was no way he could hold on.

Chapter 10

JOE WENT OVER every inch of Pickell's office with his penlight, but there was nothing there. The file was gone, the wig was missing, even the sheet of paper he had been copying when Ericson interrupted him—it had all disappeared. Brenda or Ericson must've come back and cleaned up, Joe thought angrily.

As he rifled through Pickell's desk one last time, he noticed a single message light blinking on Pickell's phone. Joe decided to listen to the message.

"Pickell. It's me," a male voice said. It sounded familiar, but Joe couldn't quite place it. "If you get this message, meet me at Harlan's twenty-four-hour convenience store at the airport entrance at midnight. I may need backup."

Joe could swear he'd heard that voice before. But where? It didn't matter, this could be just the break they needed. He hurried downstairs to find Frank.

In the cavernous production area, Joe expected to see Frank, but the room was completely dark. Funny, Joe remembered there being a little light in the room.

"Frank," Joe whispered. "Frank."

"Up here."

The voice came from above him. Joe panned his flashlight along the catwalk. "Oh, man," he said. His brother was clinging to a bracket on the edge of a ramp, his feet dangling inches above some sort of liquid-filled tank.

Joe sprinted up the catwalk steps and then to the top of the ramp.

"Frank, what is that stuff?"

"Acid," Frank answered. "Not recommended for a swim."

Fifteen feet of slippery stainless steel separated Joe from his brother. There was no way for him to go down the ramp after Frank—he'd just slide right into him and they'd both be boiled to death in seconds.

"Hurry up, Joe. I'm losing my grip." Frank tried to swing one leg up to the lip of the ramp, but it was no use. He needed all his strength just to hold on.

"Give me a second, Frank," Joe yelled. "I'll be right back."

Joe tore along the catwalk, pulling bins from the shelves. They crashed to the grating, parts spilling out everywhere. "No good," Joe murmured to himself. "No good, no good."

"Here we go." He'd ripped down a container filled with narrow gauge spars—thin aluminum tubes used to brace wing struts. Each tube was about two feet long and had a hole drilled in each end. Joe grabbed a handful and dashed back to the ramp.

"What're you doing?" Frank still sounded calm. That was good.

"Just a few more seconds."

Using the nuts and bolts spilled on the catwalk, Joe started linking spars together. Within seconds, he had eight of them bolted together to make a sixteen-foot-long aluminum rope.

"Grab on," he shouted, lowering one end of the linked tubes down to his brother. Joe knew that Frank would have to let go of the ramp to grasp the spar, so he held his end tight and braced his feet against the railing.

"I'm going for it," Frank said.

"Ready."

The makeshift rope suddenly went taut. Joe strained to hold on. Slowly, pulling hand over hand, he reeled in one section of spar at a time. He broke into a sweat. His hands got slippery.

He paused and the spar he was holding immediately began to slip from his hands.

He heard Frank call up, "What's going on, Joe?"

"I got you." With a final, tremendous effort, Joe drew in the last few spars. Frank's head appeared above the edge of the ramp.

"Thanks," Frank said. He used the railing to pull himself up. He stood on the catwalk and shook the cramps out of his tired hands.

"You've got cuts all over your face," Joe said. "What happened in here?"

"I got ambushed. Somebody hit me from behind. After he dumped me on the ramp, he poured a case filled with parts down on my head." Frank took a deep breath. "If you hadn't shown up when you did, I'd just be a pile of bones in that vat."

"Did you get a look at the guy?"

"Not his face," Frank answered. "He was strong as a gorilla. I'm pretty sure it was Buddy Berkemeier from Starkey Aviation."

"Buddy? So Brenda was right?"

"Who knows," Frank said. "They could all be in it together."

"You mean the whole crowd at Starkey Aviation?"

Frank nodded, peeked over the railing one last time, and shook his head with relief. "What'd you come up with in Pickell's office?" he asked.

"Surprise, surprise—I couldn't find the file I had out anywhere," Joe said. "But I did get something."

Frank raised his eyebrows. "What?"

"A phone call for Pickell," Joe said. "He's got an important meeting at a convenience store outside the airport in . . ." Joe pushed the illuminator button on his watch. "Seventeen minutes. Let's go."

It took Frank and Joe a little over ten minutes to jog the mile or so to the convenience store. It was almost midnight as they approached carefully from the field behind the store. The mart was open, and except for a big gas tanker truck parked beside the building, the lot was empty.

The Hardys scouted the situation thoroughly. They could see the uniformed driver of the gas truck inside chatting with the store clerk. A hose ran from the back of the truck into the underground gas storage tanks.

"Let's hide behind the truck," Frank suggested. "We can see everything from there."

"Got it."

The droning of the truck's pump drowned out everything around them. Frank had been right, though; this was the perfect lookout spot.

Moments later, at midnight, a black sedan pulled into the lot. The driver cut the lights and got out.

"It's Ericson," Joe said. "And he's got the envelope."

Ericson looked around furtively, then headed into the store.

"Now's our chance," Joe said, starting around the tanker.

"Hold on, Joe. Here comes another car."

The Hardys watched as a green car wheeled into the lot too fast. The driver didn't cut off the engine or the headlights. He pulled up in front of the store and sat there, the engine idling.

"Ericson's meeting someone," Frank said. "I wonder if it's Pickell, if our mystery caller got hold of him somewhere else."

They watched as Ericson came out of the store. He stood under the security lights for a second, hesitating, then went up to the driver's side window of the green car. Someone inside rolled the window down halfway.

"Who is it?" Joe asked. "Can you see?"

"I can't. He's wearing some kind of a mask."

The man in the car grabbed the envelope. Ericson said something they couldn't hear, and reached in, trying to take the envelope back.

"Now," Frank said.

"I'll get Ericson," Joe said, already running. "You go for the car."

There was a gunshot and a muzzle flash from inside the car. Ericson jerked back, staggered, then slumped to the blacktop.

"He's hit!" Joe shouted, rushing to the mechanic's side. He glanced into the store, trying to signal the clerk to call 911, but both the clerk and the truck driver had hit the floor.

Frank saw the driver's window power up. He pulled at the door handle. Locked. The driver had the car in reverse and was starting out of the lot. Taking a step back, Frank nailed the window with a powerful side kick. The glass spidered into a maze of cracks. Frank thrust the foot again and the window shattered into a thousand tiny bits.

He reached in for the driver. He had to get at the mask, had to see the guy's face before he got away. But all Frank saw was the barrel of a gun aimed right between his eyes.

Things seemed to move in slow motion then. The car kept backing up as Frank raised his hand to knock the gun aside. He watched the driver's knuckles whiten as he squeezed the trigger. Then Frank saw the hammer fall.

Chapter 11

Frank closed his eyes against the flash. As he fell to the ground he smelled burning gunpowder, then saw the wheel of the sedan roll past, missing him by inches.

Frank touched the tips of his fingers to his face. In the background, he heard the green sedan tear out of the parking lot, engine gunning, tires screeching. He drew his fingers away—no blood. He didn't feel right, though.

"Frank, are you hit?" Joe rushed over. He checked his brother all over for wounds.

Frank shook his head. "Just dazed, I think," he began. "My ears are ringing."

"You have powder burns all over your face."

Joe helped his brother to his feet. "Did you see who it was? Was it Pickell?"

"I couldn't get at the mask. But I don't think it was Pickell. I bet he never got the message. All I saw was the gun," he said. "A Browning Hi-Power."

"That's a cannon. You're lucky he missed."

"Joe, where's Ericson?"

Joe turned. "Right over—hey, he's gone. He must've taken off."

Frank walked over to where Ericson had fallen. "He won't get far." He gestured to a pool of blood. "It looks like he was hit pretty bad."

The convenience store clerk leaned his head cautiously out the door. "I saw everything," he said. "The cops are on the way."

Joe could already hear the sirens in the distance. "What did you see?" he asked.

"I saw the guy in the car waste that other guy," the clerk said. "That's when I ducked down."

"Then what'd you see?"

"I looked up in time to see him almost blow your head off," the clerk said, pointing at Frank. "And the plates. I saw the plates for a second. It was a rental car."

"You didn't get the number?" Frank asked.

"No, sorry, man. Just that it was a rental."

"Thanks," Joe said. "Just tell the cops what you saw, okay?" He turned to his brother.

"Come on, Frank. I don't feel like having a two-hour conversation with the police."

"I agree. Ericson could bleed to death by then."

"Hey, you can't leave," the clerk said. But the Hardys had taken off up the road toward their hotel, ducking behind a row of darkened buildings to avoid being seen.

Back in the hotel room, Joe went to the phone while Frank ran some cold water on a towel.

"Hello, County General?" Joe said into the receiver. He made himself sound busy and fed-up. "This is Detective Ryecroft speaking. I need to know if you've admitted anyone with a gunshot wound within the last twenty minutes or so. No? Well, give me a call at this number if you do." He read the number off the hotel phone. "Yes," he continued. "A young male around six feet tall. He could be armed and dangerous. Thanks." He hung up and picked the next hospital number in the book.

A few minutes later Frank came out of the bathroom. He had used the wet towel to cool the powder burns and cuts on his face. "Any luck?"

"No," Joe replied. "I've called four hospitals. No gunshot wounds."

"He could've passed out from blood loss," Frank noted. "Then we'd be looking for someone admitted for being in a car accident."

"Right," Joe said. He was just starting to call the next emergency room when someone started banging on their door.

"Who's there?" Frank asked. There was more banging.

Joe closed the phone book and went to the peephole. "It's Brenda," he said, opening the door.

Brenda grabbed Joe by the arm. "In my room," she said. "Now." It looked as if she'd been crying, but her voice was firm.

"What is it?"

"It's James. He's been shot." Making certain the hallway was clear, Brenda opened the door to her room. "He showed up fifteen minutes ago. I think he's dying."

They rushed into the room. Ericson lay on the bed, one arm dangling over the edge. He'd been shot in the right side of his chest. Blood soaked the sheets.

"He's a mess," Joe said. Ericson's shirt was open. Brenda had tried to patch him up with a hotel towel, but blood still oozed out all around.

Tears rolled down Brenda's cheeks as she leaned over her boyfriend. She cried silently, her breath catching in her throat. "I didn't know what to do," she said. "I didn't call an ambulance because the cops might come."

"We've got to call," Joe said. "He's dead if we

don't." He picked up the phone to dial 911 while Frank brought fresh towels from the bathroom.

Ericson woke when Frank put the new compress on his chest. "Brenda," he whispered.

"She's right here," Frank said.

Brenda leaned in close to Ericson. "Don't talk, James. It's going to be okay."

"No," he said. "You have to know."

"What do I have to know?"

Ericson was as pale as the pillowcase his head rested on. He tried to sit up, but Frank pushed him back down gently. "I had the evidence," he murmured. "Buddy ordered the bad parts. They framed me. They—they made your father do it, Brenda."

"I know, baby. Be quiet now."

"Made her father do what?" Frank asked. "Shoot Hutchens?"

Ericson didn't answer for a beat. Then he said, "I need a drink of water."

"Sure," Frank replied. "But who framed you, James? Who shot you?"

Brenda held a glass to Ericson's lips and helped him take a sip of water. Then he lay back again. "The NTSB," Ericson whispered. "The investigator called and said he knew I had the evidence. He said, he said . . ."

Brenda put a hand on James's shoulder. "Take your time."

"He said meet him at the convenience store. He said to bring the file with me."

"Who said that?" Frank asked. "Did you get a name?"

"I—I don't know. He was talking fast. I—I was nervous." Ericson's lips trembled.

"So you have no idea who shot you?"

"I couldn't see. He . . . had a ski mask. He grabbed the file. That's all I remember." Ericson looked at his girlfriend. "I did it for you, Brenda," he said. Then his eyes closed and his head flopped to the side.

Brenda gasped and clutched her hands over her mouth. "Is he . . ."

"No. He's not dead. He just passed out." Frank glanced up at Joe. "He walked right into a trap. Whoever called Pickell's office must've called Ericson, too."

"How could he be sure it was the NTSB who called? It could've been anybody."

Frank nodded. "He was reckless. He shouldn't have gone all alone."

"*You* were there," Brenda shouted. "Why didn't you help him?"

"We tried," Joe said. "We were supposed to be working on this together, but your boyfriend decided to go it alone."

"You let him get shot."

"Wrong. He got himself shot. And he almost got Frank killed, too," Joe said.

Before Brenda could reply, two female paramedics burst into the room pushing a gurney and a crash cart. They went to work on Ericson while the Hardys and Brenda stepped out into the hall to talk to the police.

While one officer interviewed them, another followed the medics inside. Brenda kept trying to look back into her hotel room. It was a long five minutes before the paramedics wheeled Ericson out.

"How is he?" Brenda asked.

One paramedic held an oxygen mask over Ericson's mouth while the other hooked an IV plasma drip on a hanger. "He's stabilized," the first medic said. She turned to the officer interviewing the teens. "Can she ride with us?"

"Go on," the officer said.

Brenda gratefully followed her boyfriend down the hall and into the elevator. The first officer stopped his partner as he walked by. "Keep an eye on her," he said. "And if the kid wakes up, get a statement."

When the hall cleared out, the officer, a square-jawed, earnest-looking guy not much older than the Hardys, proceeded to ask Frank and Joe a few more questions, including why they'd left the shooting scene earlier.

"We knew our friend was hit," Frank stated. "We had to find him."

The officer nodded, making notes. Finally he

seemed satisfied. "Don't leave town without calling the station," he said. "We may have more questions for you later."

"No problem," Frank replied.

Back in their room, Joe opened a can of soda for himself and tossed one to Frank. "Have some sugar and caffeine," he said. "You look like you could use it."

Frank caught the can and sat down on his bed. "I guess even you'll have to admit Ericson looks pretty innocent now," he said.

"Just because he got shot? I'm not so sure." Joe sat on the low dresser. "You don't really think it was the NTSB that called him, do you?"

Frank took a swig of soda. "No way."

"If Ericson had just stayed back in Bayport we'd have all this wrapped up by now. He just got in the way."

"He was watching out for Brenda, or I guess that's what he thought."

They heard a voice from out in the hall—"Hello"—followed by a knock on their door. "Frank and Joe Hardy, are you in?"

Joe gave his brother a look that said, "Who could that be at this hour?"

As if reading his thoughts, the voice boomed out, "It's Investigator Mitchell. Open the door now."

Joe let Mitchell in. He was dressed as nattily as ever, even though it was almost 1:00 A.M. He wore a dark gray suit and a perfectly pressed white shirt.

He strode to the center of the room and motioned for Joe to sit on the bed next to his brother.

"No, thanks. I'll stand," Joe said.

Mitchell set his briefcase on the dresser and crossed his arms. "What are you boys doing here?" he asked.

Joe shrugged. "Nothing much. Just checking out the Cajun food."

"Very funny. I tried calling you in Bayport to give you an update on the case—like I promised I would. What do I find out? That you're down here trying to get yourselves killed. I just heard all the details from the local police."

"Thanks for your concern," Joe said, taking a gulp of his drink. "But we're fine."

"Fine?" Mitchell pointed at Joe. "You may be fine, young man, but I am conducting an official investigation and I had all the evidence I needed. Now it's gone, missing because you came down here, interfered, and spooked Ericson and Pickell."

Frank stood up. "What kind of evidence?"

"First, you tell me what Ericson said tonight. He's going directly into surgery and I didn't get to ask him any questions."

Frank was careful not to give away too much. He wanted to see what cards Mitchell held first. "He just told Brenda that he did it for her," Frank said.

"Yep," Joe chimed in. "He said it several times: 'I did it for you, Brenda.' "

"That's it?"

"That's it," Joe answered. "He passed out before we could ask him what he meant."

Mitchell put his hands in his pockets. "Okay," he said. "That fits with what I've got. Now, I'm telling you this only so you'll get out of my hair, right?"

The Hardys both nodded.

"Here's what I can prove so far: that Hutchens and Ericson were running the scam. Starkey knowingly bought the bad parts—at first to keep costs down, later because Hutchens blackmailed him. And young Brenda Starkey isn't totally innocent either. She may have set the whole thing up. She brought Ericson in, and together they hatched this plan to keep her father's company running."

"So who shot Ericson tonight?" Frank asked.

Mitchell picked up his briefcase. "That I don't know," he said. "I think these crooks are starting to get nervous and turn against one another. First Starkey murders Hutchens, now somebody tries to silence Ericson."

"That means I'm clear," Frank said. "The crash wasn't my fault, so I'll get my license back."

"Right," Mitchell said. Now he seemed in a hurry to leave. He headed for the door, then turned back. "Listen closely to what I'm about to say, Frank. If you two don't catch the earliest flight back to Bayport tomorrow, you'll never get your license back. I hate to play hardball like this, but that's the way it has to be, understood?"

"Okay," Frank said. "I get it."

After Joe had closed the door behind Mitchell, Frank wandered over to the window. He could see the parking lot three stories below, illuminated by rows of tall, phosphorescent street lamps.

"What do you think?" Joe asked. "Are we heading back home in the morning?"

"No way," Frank said. "We're too close. And Mitchell can't make good on his threat unless I do something wrong."

Joe clapped his brother on the back. "That's what I like to hear, Frank."

There were only a few cars arriving at the Baton Rouge airport that time of night. In the distance Frank could see the control tower. The radar dish on top spun steadily around, searching the empty skies.

"There's Mitchell now," Joe said.

Sure enough, Mitchell appeared from under

the hotel entrance awning and disappeared into a shadowy corner of the parking lot.

Seconds later headlights came on and a car pulled out under the row of streetlamps.

"Hey, do you see what I see?" Joe asked.

"Mitchell's car," Frank said. "It's the green sedan from the convenience store!"

Chapter 12

"WHICH MEANS *Mitchell's* the one who shot Ericson?" Joe said in disbelief.

"It sure looks that way," Frank said. "But we can't be sure. He didn't have a hair out of place."

"Some people can pull it off," Joe said. "Shoot another person in cold blood, then put on a happy face as if nothing happened."

Frank turned away from the window and pulled the shades closed. "We still need hard evidence. It could just be a coincidence that Mitchell's car is the same."

"Oh, right," Joe said, with a cynical half smile. "The rental car companies here in Baton Rouge *only* have green cars?"

Frank ignored the comment. "I say we go back

to Pickell one more time and toss the place," he said. "I'm sure we'll turn something up."

"Let's go," Joe said.

"First, we let things cool down," Frank said. "Tomorrow's Sunday. The plant will be closed. Besides, I could use some sleep. Let's set the alarm for five and then head over there."

Four hours later, dressed in dark clothes, the Hardys sneaked back into Pickell Machine Works. The moon had set, and it was the darkest part of the night, just before dawn. A few birds were waking up, starting to sing and call across the fields surrounding the airport.

Frank discovered that the window he'd used earlier was still open.

"I guess Buddy wasn't too concerned about how we got in," Joe said.

Frank climbed through the opening, then motioned for Joe to follow. "I think Buddy figures I'm liquefied," he whispered.

This time they scoured Pickell's office from top to bottom. Joe found a stack of playing cards in Pickell's closet, along with poker chips and matchbooks from several riverboat casinos on the Mississippi. "Looks like Pickell's tried his luck on a few boats other than the *Proud Mary,*" he said.

"There's no law against gambling," Frank said.

"True, but it can be a pretty strong motivator to make fast money."

"Got something," Frank said. He stood up behind Pickell's desk. "A bank book."

Joe watched as Frank scanned the columns with his penlight. "There are some pretty hefty withdrawals," Frank said.

Joe counted back the dates on his fingers. "They occur every Monday like clockwork," he said. "Pickell could be paying off weekend gambling debts."

"No way to tell without the canceled checks," Frank noted. "But here's something interesting."

"What?" Joe asked.

"Remember the dates of the three crashes of the planes from Starkey?" Joe nodded. "Look at this," Frank said, running his finger down the columns of the passbook. "Two very big payments shortly after each crash."

"Like they're bribing someone to keep quiet?"

"Exactly."

"Make copies," Joe said, moving toward the door. "I'll keep watch."

Frank made the copies quickly, then they checked the other offices along the hallway.

"Looks like Jerry Cook's office to me," Joe said when they came back to one right next to Pickell's. The quality control supervisor's walls were covered with poster-size squares of cork-board. Tacked to the boards were computer printouts of charts with row upon row of numbers.

Frank pored over the charts. "This makes it look like they analyze every batch of their parts," he said.

"It looks good for the customers," Joe said.

"They must do two separate runs of each part. They show the good parts to the NTSB, and they sell the bad parts to Starkey."

"And maybe other companies," Joe said. "Who knows how big this thing is."

Frank nodded. "As long as they have inside help—a mechanic at the company and someone inside the government to cover their tracks," he said. "They must be making a mint."

Joe closed the drawers of Cook's desk. "And if anyone ever gets too close to figuring it out, they dissolve the evidence in those acid vats," he said.

Frank went to the file cabinets behind the desk. "Cook seems like the kind of guy who'd save every piece of paper he ever handled. Maybe that's how we can trip him up."

He flipped through each file, noting the customer names and dates of delivery. Anytime he saw something interesting, he handed it to Joe to read, then continued his search. The first hint of daylight was beginning to show through the shades.

Frank handed Joe a file marked Complaints.

Joe stood by the window, reading. "It's just

return orders from customers who got the wrong parts," he said finally.

Frank replaced the file and tried to close the cabinet, but the drawer jammed.

"Something's ripping," Joe warned.

Frank pulled the file drawer back out and peered in. "I can't see what it's stuck on."

"Pull it all the way out." Joe put down his flashlight and helped his brother remove the entire drawer. They set it on the desk.

"Good call," Frank said. He reached up under the top panel of the file cabinet and pulled out a thick manila folder. "Somebody deliberately taped this to the inside of the cabinet."

Frank flipped through the sheaf of documents in the folder as Joe peered over his shoulder. "Look at these," he said, handing some to Joe. "Aren't they what you found in Pickell's office earlier?"

Joe nodded. "Letters from Hutchens to Pickell Machine Works. Here's one from almost a year ago." He read aloud: " 'E. is on board. S.A. will buy twenty-five thousand dollars of special value parts per month. Ten percent will cover my expenses. Have list of new prospects in New York area.' "

"E. must be Ericson," Frank said. "And S.A. would be Starkey Aviation."

"Right," Joe agreed. "Hutchens was taking ten percent of the total orders in kickbacks."

"There's more." Frank produced a black leather-bound accounting ledger. Inside, in what they could only guess was Cook's meticulous handwriting, were records of deposits and withdrawals from several different accounts. Brenda Starkey's name showed up on more than a few of the deposit entries.

"See, she had you fooled, Frank. I knew all along we couldn't trust her."

Frank let out a whistle. "You were right. And here are some entries recording payments to Hutchens, Ericson, and Berkemeier. They were all on the secret payroll."

Joe handed the Hutchens letter back to Frank. "Looks like we've got the evidence we need—case closed," he said.

Then Joe saw the frown on his brother's face. "What is it, Frank?"

"I'm not sure, but hold on a second. . . ." Frank pulled a ragged piece of paper from the back pocket of his jeans. He carefully unfolded it and placed it beside the letter they'd just found. In response to Joe's quizzical expression, Frank said, "It's my suspension letter from Hutchens. I've been carrying it around for the past few days. I must've read it a dozen times."

"So?"

"So look at the signatures." Frank pointed them out. The one on his letter was a slanted scrawl, barely legible. The one on the letter from the folder was a pretty good imitation, but more upright and much neater. "They're different," he said. "One of them's got to be a forgery."

Joe raised his eyebrows. "This one's too neat," he said, picking up the incriminating letter. "It's almost as if whoever wrote it wanted to make sure we could read the name."

"Exactly. This is all too easy," Frank said.

"You mean this is phony evidence?"

Frank nodded grimly. "It's definitely a setup," he said.

"But who's setting up who?"

"That's what we've got to find out," Frank said.

At that moment the window shades glowed bright, then quickly darkened, as if a spotlight had passed over them.

"What was that?" Frank whispered.

Joe peered around the edge of the shade. "A car," he said. "Three men are getting out. There's Pickell . . . Cook's getting out now. And there's your friend Buddy."

Frank put the papers back in the folder. "We're taking this," he said, "fake or not."

The Hardys quickly replaced the file drawer.

Joe led the way down the hall, pausing at the top of the stairs. Voices drifted up toward them from the darkness below. "They're on their way up," he said.

"Just keep on going down the stairs. We don't want to get trapped upstairs."

The lights went on downstairs, and the voices grew louder. They recognized Cook's voice above the others.

Frank and Joe crept down the stairs slowly, pausing on the lower landing. They could see the three men standing in a triangle in the middle of the entrance hall.

Cook pointed toward the production area. "Buddy," he said, "you go take care of the special orders."

Pickell was upset. "You know how much that's going to cost us, Jerry?"

"Do you want to spend twenty-five years in prison? We've got to get rid of that stuff and lay low for a while."

Pickell sucked on a cigarette, then flicked it down to the floor. "I don't like it," he muttered. "There's no reason for this."

Cook gave Pickell a hard stare. He bent down and picked up the cigarette butt. "You'll thank me for this later," he said.

"All right, sure. Let's just get on with it."

Buddy headed for the factory floor. Pickell and Cook walked directly toward where the Hardys were hiding.

As Joe pivoted to go back up the stairs, he slipped and pitched forward. He managed to break his fall with his hands, but the sound of his palms slapping the carpeted steps was loud enough.

"What was that?" Pickell shouted. He and Cook rushed to the stairs.

"Go, Frank." Joe scrambled up the steps after his brother. He glanced back and saw Pickell at the bottom of the stairs, pulling a .45 automatic from under his shirt.

As Joe reached the upstairs hallway, the wall in front of him seemed to explode. A white cloud of plaster stung his face. The next shot hit six inches lower, but Joe had already made the turn down the hall.

Seeing Frank dart into Pickell's office, Joe followed. He could hear their pursuers climbing the stairs.

"They're trapped now," Pickell was saying. "There's no place they can go."

Once Joe was in the office, Frank slammed the door shut. "Give me that chair," he yelled.

Joe tossed Pickell's office chair to his brother, who jammed it under the doorknob.

"How long will that slow them down?"

"I don't know," Frank said. "Let me think."

They saw the knob turn. Someone on the outside slammed into the door, but it didn't budge. The crisp report of the .45 followed, and a hole the size of a golf ball opened up over the knob.

"Okay, Frank. Thinking time's up."

There was another shot, this one blowing the knob right out of the door.

Frank rushed to the side window and ripped aside the shade. He took a step back and with a flying kick shattered the glass, then stuck his head out the window. "We jump," he said.

Joe looked out the window as a third shot almost tore the door in half. He could see a Dumpster on the ground below. "It must be twenty feet down," he said.

"It's a bullet or a fall," Frank replied. "Take your pick." Shielding his face with his arms from the shards of glass, he took a flying leap.

Chapter 13

Joe heard a loud crash as his brother landed, but he didn't dare look down. He put one leg through the window, hesitated just long enough to see Pickell burst through the office door, and jumped.

The fall seemed to occur in slow motion to Joe. Crashing into the Dumpster feet first, he concentrated on letting his body fold and roll, as he'd been taught in his sky-diving classes. He hit so hard that his legs collapsed under him and he bounced back up a few feet. When he landed again he rolled forward, taking the sting out of the impact. His head slammed into something hard.

"Ouch." Frank sat in a pile of crushed cardboard boxes, holding his palm to his eye socket. "You head-butted me, Joe."

"Sorry." Joe felt as if he were swimming in cardboard. "You're lucky I didn't land right on top of you."

"I'm counting my blessings." Frank scrambled out of the Dumpster, pulling his brother after him.

They heard Pickell fire at them again. The bullet ricocheted off the rim of the Dumpster and whirred off into the distance.

"Hold it right there," Pickell shouted. "You move and I'll waste you."

But the Hardys weren't about to stop. They took off along the wall of the building, Pickell's gunshots biting into the pavement behind them.

Frank ducked around the corner. He found himself in a narrow alley formed by the back wall of PMW and a storage warehouse behind it. Once Joe was safe there, too, they stopped to catch their breath. They could hear Pickell cursing up in his office.

"You okay?" Frank asked.

Joe brushed bits of foam packing peanuts from the front of his shirt. "Just fine," he said. "You?"

"Except for a possible black eye, I'm terrific."

The sun was now coming up over the horizon at one end of the alley. Off in the distance a 727 taxied into takeoff position, turning slowly in the reddish light, its engines hissing and roaring.

"Think anyone heard those gunshots over the jet engines?" Joe asked.

"I doubt it. Come on, let's clear out."

"You've got to get past me first," a voice behind them said.

It was Buddy. The short, barrel-chested mechanic stepped out of a side door and faced them, his huge hands dangling at his sides.

Joe put the manila folder down and raised his fists. Frank took two steps to the side, putting some distance between himself and Joe, and assumed a fighting stance.

Buddy just grimaced, showing his big teeth, and came straight at them. He charged Frank first, and Joe heard the thump and watched as his brother fell backward. Buddy came on like Frankenstein's monster, picking Frank up off the ground and shaking him hard.

Joe stepped in and landed a crushing right hook to Buddy's jaw. It was a punch that would have knocked most men down, but the sturdy mechanic just dropped Frank and staggered back a few feet.

Joe knew he had to press his advantage, no matter how small it was. He faked another punch to Buddy's face, then stomped on the inside arch of the man's foot. This time Buddy howled in pain.

Back on his feet, Frank measured the distance and whirled into a roundhouse kick, catching

Buddy over his right ear and finally putting him on his knees.

Joe prepared to deliver one more blow, when he felt something cold and hard against his temple. He froze, raising his hands over his head.

"That's enough, fellows." It was Cook, with a .45 automatic just like Pickell's. He gave Buddy a minute or two to recover. Then, after grabbing the evidence folder from Joe, the two of them marched the Hardys back into the building.

Inside, Pickell took the folder from Cook. "What have we here?" he said. He held one hand to his mouth, stifling a cough, then opened the file. "What? Where'd you get this?"

The Hardys kept quiet.

"What is this, Jerry?" Pickell handed the stack of papers to Cook.

Cook scowled. "There's enough evidence in here to send the three of us to prison for a long time," he said. "But what's this?" He held up the letter from Hutchens. He read it aloud, then handed it to Pickell.

Pickell got right in Frank's face. "Where did you find this?"

Frank stared off into the distance.

The old man faced Cook. "You know what this means, don't you?"

Cook nodded, but Pickell didn't seem to notice, continuing to go off on a tirade. "It means," he said, "that we've been set up. Our so-called silent partner planted this because he plans for us to take the fall, and he's rigged it so Hutchens goes down in his place."

Cook nodded toward the Hardys. "Quiet, Bob," he warned. "We don't know how much they know yet."

"It doesn't matter how much they know," Pickell growled, waving the gun in the air. "It's over. All of it."

Frank figured he had nothing to lose. He decided to try to confirm his hunch. "We've got it worked out," he said. "We know this is fake evidence and we have proof that it was Mitchell, not Hutchens, who was your inside man."

"Well, aren't you just so smart?" Pickell sneered.

Cook shifted from one foot to the other. "Quiet, Bob. There's still a way out of this."

"Sure there's a way out of it," Pickell said, holding the .45 under Frank's chin. "First, we burn that folder. Second, we boil all the bad parts down to scrap. Third, we take care of these two. And last but not least, we fix that pretty-boy Mitchell."

"Now, hold on a second. Don't you think that's a little extreme?" Cook asked.

This time Buddy piped up. "It's got to be done, Jerry." Cook turned toward him with his gun. Ignoring the gun, Buddy wrapped a big hand around the thin man's throat and pulled him close. "If you don't want to die with them, you do what the boss says, got it?"

"Okay, okay," Cook said. "Just make it quick and clean."

Pickell waved the Hardys ahead with his pistol and the five of them entered the production warehouse. Inside, he flipped on the overhead lights. "Buddy," he said. "Start dumping parts. As soon as you're done, we add these two to the mix."

Buddy climbed the stairs to the catwalk and began noisily dumping entire bins of parts down the steel ramp and into the acid vat. A silver fog rose to the ceiling, filling the room with a horrible smell.

"Come on, step lively," Pickell said to the Hardys. He prodded Joe with the barrel of his gun.

It was all Joe could do to control himself. He knew he could take Pickell, even with the gun, but now wasn't the time. He had to be patient. He had to wait for the signal from Frank.

"Get up on the edge of the vat," Pickell said. He forced the teens to kneel right beside the glass-lined wall of the acid bath, hands clasped behind their heads. He stood behind Frank, while Cook anxiously guarded Joe.

All four of them watched as Buddy dragged bin after bin of parts to the ramp and dumped them out. Nuts, bolts, aluminum struts, brake shoes, clamps, connecting rods, fans, hundreds of different parts slid into the acid, hissing as they hit.

A heavy engine part plunked into the acid with a splash, sending a shower of drops toward the Hardys. Watching them duck and wince, Pickell chuckled. "Jump in," he said, "the water's fine."

Joe glanced at his brother. Frank seemed to be silently saying, "Be patient."

Pickell stopped laughing and snorted, clearing his throat. "I need a cigarette," he announced to no one in particular. He stuck his pistol in his waistband and tapped out a smoke from his pack.

Now was the time. Frank made his move, back-handing Pickell in the gut. The old man's cigarettes flew up and into the acid pit as he fell backward, dropping his gun.

Instantly, Cook hammered Frank with the butt of his gun, sending him reeling.

Joe jumped on Cook, landing on his back like a cougar. They both landed hard on the cement floor. He had to get Cook's gun, that was all that mattered. Digging his knee into Cook's back, Joe forced the weaker man's wrist behind his back. Cook dropped the .45 and Joe kicked it aside.

He lifted Cook to a standing position, only to see Pickell crawling after his gun. Off to the side, Frank was still recovering from Cook's blow.

"Watch it, Frank," Joe shouted.

Frank made a move toward Pickell just as the old man reached his pistol. Still on his knees, Pickell pulled back the slide on the automatic and fired wildly.

Over the blast, Joe heard a woman's horrified scream.

Chapter 14

PICKELL FIRED AGAIN, the recoil from the big .45 making his whole arm jump. Frank lowered his head and drove his shoulder into the older man's rib cage. The gun discharged again, blasting a hole high in the ceiling. Pickell collapsed in a heap, and a shaft of light burst through and lit up the floor like a laser beam.

Grabbing Pickell's gun hand, Frank easily wrenched the pistol away and tossed it into the dissolving pool. Frank didn't stand over the old man and gloat. He spun around quickly, ready to defend himself against another attacker. But Buddy was still up on the catwalk, staring down at the scene below. It was Brenda who had screamed as she stood in the entrance at the far end.

Then Frank noticed Joe, who was kneeling beside Cook, his fingers at the man's throat.

"What happened?" Frank asked.

"No pulse," Joe said. "He's dead."

"Pickell?"

Joe nodded. "It looks like the boss shot him right in the heart. I had him with his arm behind his back. All of a sudden he just collapsed."

Blood had pooled around Cook's body, spreading in every direction.

Pickell went pale. "No," he mumbled. "I didn't do that. I can't believe it."

"Come on down, Buddy," Frank called. "It's over. We're calling the cops."

Brenda's quavering voice said differently. "Frank, I'm sorry," she called across the warehouse. Her voice was barely strong enough to carry that distance. "It's not over yet."

Frank and Joe watched as Mitchell stepped through the doorway, holding a gun to Brenda's head.

"Look what I found leaving the hospital," Mitchell said, shoving Brenda ahead of him. "Our little insurance policy."

"Let her go," Joe said angrily.

"I don't think so, tough guy. You're going to do exactly what I tell you from now on."

As Mitchell moved closer, Frank noticed that his gun was the same one used at the convenience store—a Browning Hi-Power. If Mitchell had already tried to kill Ericson, there was no reason he wouldn't shoot Brenda. "Stay cool, Joe," he said.

"That's right," Mitchell said. "Listen to your brother. He's obviously the smart one." The NTSB supervisor forced Brenda to stop a few yards from the Hardys. He kept the gun leveled at the back of her head.

Pickell staggered over, staring blankly. He pointed at Mitchell. "You coward," he said. "You planted that file to set us up."

Mitchell shouted up at Buddy, "Keep dumping those parts, Berkemeier. As soon as you're done, we're out of here."

"Don't ignore me," Pickell shouted. "Why did you do it?" He turned suddenly and faced Frank. "Tell me now—where did you find that file?"

Frank hesitated. Here was his chance to set Pickell and Mitchell against each other. "We found the file in Cook's office," he said. "It was taped to the inside of the file cabinet."

"Just obvious enough so someone searching the office would find it," Joe added.

"What were you going to do," Pickell shouted at Mitchell, "make an anonymous call to the cops? Was that the plan? They come and find the evidence that puts us away while you go free."

"Listen, you old fool," Mitchell said. "If you hadn't gambled all our money away, we'd be living off it in South America by now."

"You betrayed us," Pickell spat out.

"No, I had everything worked out. Only Hutchens and Ericson were going down. Then you got careless and I had to protect myself."

"You're good at that, aren't you?" Joe said.

"You're the one who beat Hutchens to death," Frank added. "Not Starkey."

"That's enough out of you," Mitchell said. "I'm not going to answer that." He pointed his Browning at Pickell. "Go pick up Cook's gun, old man. We've got some cleanup to do. Then we'll go our separate ways. I'll disappear and you can spend every single night on the *Proud Mary* if you want."

Pickell stayed planted.

"Do it," Mitchell yelled. "Or I'll put a bullet in your head right now."

Pickell reluctantly walked over to where Joe had kicked Cook's .45. He picked the gun up but held it as if it were a dead mouse he'd just found under his kitchen sink.

"Come on," Mitchell said. "We're all going on a little airplane flight. Buddy will be done frying all the parts by the time we get back."

Mitchell reached into a side pocket of his suit coat and pulled out a roll of duct tape. He tossed it to Pickell. "Bind their wrists," he ordered. "And do a good job of it."

Then, still holding the gun to Brenda's head, Mitchell marched them all out to the PMW taxiway. The sun was up now, and off in the distance the airport terminal was bustling with activity. They could see fuel trucks and baggage tractors zipping back and forth between the terminal building and thc jets.

A small twin-engine plane sat ready on the taxiway. "Pickell," Mitchell said. "You take the pilot's seat." He motioned for the Hardys to climb into the back of the plane. Then he got in himself, pushing Brenda ahead of him.

The three teenagers sat in a row against one wall of the little plane. Mitchell hunched against the opposite wall, his lanky body cramped in the tight space. "Let's go," he shouted to Pickell.

The twin props roared to life, and Pickell guided the plane out onto the runway. Within minutes they'd been cleared for takeoff.

"Head south," Mitchell yelled over the rattle of the engines. "Fly over the swamp near Choctaw."

Frank felt the plane accelerate and take off. They headed east, into the sun. Then they swung around and headed south, still climbing.

Brenda had her jaw set firmly. "Why did you set my father up as Hutchens's killer?" she asked.

Mitchell chuckled. "It was too easy," he said. "Or else I'm just too clever."

"What's so clever about framing a desperate man?" Joe asked.

Mitchell smiled. "Hutchens was starting to

figure things out," he said. "And after the two of you interrupted Buddy while he was pulling the broken engine mounts off the wreckage at the NTSB hangar, I knew Hutchens would finally have the evidence he needed."

"So you killed him," Frank said.

"I was just going to check his office and see how much he knew," Mitchell said, "but he'd taken his files out, hidden everything."

Joe glanced at Frank. So that's why Hutchens's office had been so totally empty.

"It would've been much neater if I could have just destroyed his files and fired him for incompetence," Mitchell continued. "But he didn't cooperate."

Pickell's voice crackled over the plane's intercom. "We're ten miles from Choctaw."

Mitchell pointed the Browning at Brenda lazily. "That's when I got your father involved. I called him up and pretended I was Hutchens. I told him to meet me right away. When he showed up, I waited until he went inside. I planted the bad engine mounts in his car, then I called the cops and told them I saw your dad leaving the scene."

"You had it all worked out," Brenda said.

"Your father was a better patsy than I could have wished for," Mitchell said. "I was hoping the engine mounts and my eyewitness testimony would be enough to get him arrested. How was

I to know he'd get Hutchens's blood all over himself? It was too perfect."

"And I guess you have a perfect plan for us?" Frank said. He wanted to keep Mitchell talking. As long as the NTSB man was distracted, Frank could work on loosening the tape around his wrists.

"That's right," Mitchell answered. "You see, we're flying over a swamp right now. The old man and I will bail out, and you three will plunge deep into the muck. I doubt if they'll find you or much of the plane. That's why I'm going to gamble and leave your wrists taped. But when the FAA and NTSB investigate, they will find two things."

"What?" Frank asked.

Mitchell held up one finger. "First, that you, Frank Hardy, were flying a stolen plane. And second, that you were flying on a suspended license. They'll conclude it was pilot error again. A tragic end for the Hardy brothers and young Brenda Starkey."

"We're over Choctaw now," Pickell said from up front.

Mitchell stood up as much as he could under the low ceiling of the plane and headed for the cockpit. He pulled a parachute from its clamp behind the copilot's seat and strapped it on. "Time to get out, Pickell," he said.

The old man abandoned the controls and

crawled between the two front seats. He put on his chute, then stood there quietly, looking haggard.

Mitchell pulled on a latch and the side door dropped open. A gust of wind howled into the plane, rattling the passenger cabin.

With exaggerated politeness, Mitchell motioned for Pickell to jump. The old man stood by the door for a second, letting the wind whip at his hair. Then suddenly he was gone, as if he'd been sucked out of the plane.

Mitchell fired two shots into the instrument panel, sending a shower of sparks through the cabin. He turned and looked back at the teenagers. "Just to be sure," he shouted as he jammed the yoke forward, ducked, and disappeared out the door.

The engines sputtered, then went silent. Suddenly the only sound was the whistling wind as the plane headed straight for the vast swamp below.

Chapter 15

"No!" Brenda yelled, a look of terror on her face.

"I can't get my hands free," Frank said. "The tape's too tight."

The plane's nose took a sheer dip toward the earth. The wind was rushing into the cabin with hurricane force now, buffeting the fuselage and shaking the whole aircraft.

Frank managed to stand up. He had to work to keep his balance as the plane continued to plummet.

"Frank," Joe said. "Can you knock that fire extinguisher off the wall?" The wind seemed to snatch the words right out of his mouth.

Frank stumbled forward a few steps. Crouching

down, he brought his shoulder up under the extinguisher, freeing it from its clamp.

"Kick it to me," Joe called. The red canister came skittering across the floor.

"Hurry up," Brenda yelled. "We've only got a few seconds left."

Bumping from one wall to the other, Frank staggered to the pilot's seat. He plopped down and wedged his knees under the yoke. The plane began to level out.

"Joe, I need help," he called. "This only buys us time."

Joe pulled the extinguisher behind him. Scraping his bound wrists against the sharp edge of the handle, he got a tear started in the duct tape. With a few powerful tugs, the tape ripped through and he was free. He rushed up front, grabbed his brother's wrists, and ripped off the tape.

His hands free, Frank went to work on the instrument panel. "Oh, man," he said. "This is a serious mess. All we can do is try to keep her level."

They were still losing altitude fast. Below them the desolate swamp loomed. Scrub trees, stumps, and patches of thick, green algae on the surface of the still water came into view.

"What's happening?" Brenda cried. "Why can't you start the engines?"

"Hang on," Frank yelled. They were a hundred feet up and falling fast.

Tree branches slapped the fuselage and wings of the plane. The windshield shattered and Joe threw his hands up to cover his face.

Frank hung on to the yoke to keep the nose up.

The plane hit the water with a terrific smack and skipped like a stone. Seconds later they hit again. The landing gear caught on something and the plane rolled, tumbling across the surface like a fallen water-skier.

Joe tucked into the crash position, covering his head with his hands. He could feel himself slamming into the door and then the instrument panel.

Finally the plane shuttered to a halt. For a second there was an eerie silence. Then came the sound of rushing water.

"We're sinking," Brenda said. "We've got to get out."

Joe looked out his window. The right wing was missing. The plane had broken up on impact and was already half-submerged. He looked to his left. Frank was gone. His door was torn from its hinges.

"Frank," Joe called. But there was no answer. He must've been thrown from the plane while it was skipping across the swamp, Joe thought.

The water was up to Joe's chest now.

"Joe, help me," Brenda said. Joe half climbed, half swam back between the pilots' seats. Her hands were still bound behind her back, and she was trying desperately to keep her head above the rising water.

Joe made it to her as the plane went under completely and everything went dark.

"Stay calm," Joe said. "There's an air pocket in here. Try to breathe normally."

"Okay," Brenda said, but she was gulping all the air she could get.

A few seconds later, the plane came to rest on the slimy bottom. "That's it," Joe said, unstrapping the tape from around her wrists. "Now we swim out."

"It's too dark. We won't make it."

"We've got to try. We're running out of air." With that, Joe clutched Brenda by the arm and dove underwater, dragging her behind him. With his free hand, he searched the wall of the plane, finally finding an open door and swimming through. Something—an underwater vine or a fish, Joe didn't know what—brushed against his face. He kept kicking until he saw the sun-dappled surface above them. Seconds later they finally broke the surface, gasping for air.

"Joe!"

"Frank, you're okay." Joe spotted his brother swimming toward them.

"It's a good thing you came up on your own,"

Frank said, relief showing on his face. "I thought the plane sank farther over there. I've been diving for you for three or four minutes."

"Which way is solid ground?" Joe said. "I don't like the idea of treading water with a bunch of alligators and snakes."

The Hardys and Brenda struggled up onto a slippery bank. Joe figured Brenda would need a few minutes to rest, but she stood up almost immediately, indicating she was ready to go.

After a twenty-minute hike through marshes and muddy bogs, they came to a county highway. Joe scratched at his arms. "I thought those mosquitoes were going to eat us alive in there."

"They were as big as sparrows," Frank said. He pointed up the road. "This way. We need to go north."

Each time a car passed, Frank stuck out his thumb, hoping for a ride. No one stopped. The way they looked, Frank wasn't surprised.

Two or three miles later, the teens heard a rumbling coming from behind them. Looking back, they saw an old, rusted-out pickup barreling down the road. Frank didn't have much hope, but he jammed his thumb in the air anyway.

The driver slammed on the brakes, coming to a stop next to the Hardys. An old farmer and his wife sat in the truck, grinning.

"What happened to y'all?" the farmer asked.

"We were out canoeing," Joe replied.

"And you dumped it, huh?"

Joe nodded. "We dumped it."

The farmer adjusted his baseball cap, as if preparing to drive very fast. "Well, jump on in back," he said. "We'll get you back to town so's you can dry off."

And the farmer did drive fast.

"He must be doing seventy-five," Frank shouted over the gusting wind.

"At least we'll be dry by the time we get there," Joe said.

Brenda clutched the walls of the truck bed, bracing herself. "We're going back to Pickell Machine Works, right?" she asked. It was the first time she'd spoken since they'd escaped from the plane. Her jaw was set, and not a hint of fear showed on her face. "We're going after Mitchell, right?"

"Right," Joe shouted.

"Good." Brenda didn't say anything else for the rest of the ride.

They had the farmer drop them off at a house close to the airport. They didn't explain that it wasn't their house; they just waited until the pickup pulled out of sight and then started walking in the direction of the control tower.

Brenda followed the Hardys as they crept up on PMW. Peeking around the corner of the building, Frank held up his hand, motioning for the other two to stop.

"I see Mitchell and Pickell," he whispered. "It looks like they're loading a plane."

"Where's Buddy?" Joe asked.

"I don't see him. He must be inside."

"I say we take care of Mitchell and the old man before big Buddy shows," Joe said.

"I'll take Mitchell," Frank said.

Brenda tapped Frank on the shoulder. "What about me?"

"Watch the door," Frank said. "If Buddy comes out, let us know."

The Hardys waited until both Mitchell and Pickell were inside the plane arranging crates. Then they sprinted onto the airfield.

They were only ten yards from the plane when Pickell stuck his head out the cargo door. His jaw dropped in surprise. A look of panic washed over his face and he took off, running from the plane.

"Get him, Joe," Frank shouted.

Joe veered after the older man, tackling him easily. One quick shot to the jaw put Pickell out.

Frank was at the door to the plane when he heard Brenda's warning shout. He stopped in his tracks and turned. There was Buddy.

Joe heard the cough and sputter of the plane's engine coming to life. Mitchell had slammed the door shut and was beginning to taxi toward the runway.

"He's getting away," Brenda yelled.

Without thinking, Joe chased after the plane, dove, and landed on a wing.

Mitchell pushed the throttle forward, accelerating, and the backwash from the prop almost blew Joe off. He held on tight. Blind to the pain he knew would follow, Joe smashed his fist through the window and reached in.

Mitchell swerved to the right, sending Joe reeling. If he pitched forward, he'd be ground to hamburger by the spinning propeller.

Regaining his balance, Joe went for Mitchell again. This time, the NTSB man was ready. He had his gun out and blasted at Joe through the shattered window.

Frank heard the gunshot. His instinct was to run and make sure Joe was okay, but now he had to deal with Big Buddy Birkemeier.

The mechanic approached more cautiously this time. When he was a few feet away, he produced a three-foot-long steel rod from behind his back. He grinned and took a deadly swipe at Frank's head.

Frank ducked and darted to the side. Buddy might be stronger, but Frank was quicker. He nailed the fat man with a knee to the kidneys.

Buddy yowled in pain. He pivoted like a hitter turning on a curveball and swung at Frank again. Frank bobbed and weaved like a boxer, working to stay away from the rod and get inside and inflict some punishment.

"Over here, Frank." Brenda caught Frank's attention and tossed him a rod just like Buddy's.

"Now this seems like a fair fight," Frank said with a smile.

Buddy wasn't amused. He lifted his weapon over his head and brought it down in a chopping motion.

Frank blocked the blow, and with lightning fast moves, jabbed the aluminum rod into Buddy's gut, then snapped it up under his chin.

The mechanic's eyes rolled back and he pitched forward, unconscious.

Frank immediately turned his attention to his brother. But Mitchell's plane was at least a quarter mile down the runway now. And there was Joe clinging to the wing like a crazy stuntman.

Joe ducked away from the window. Mitchell's shot had missed him, but it clipped the tip of the wing, taking off a big splotch of paint.

The plane was nearing takeoff speed now. Peering in the window, Joe saw Mitchell drop the gun, take the yoke with two hands, and pull back. The plane lifted into the air.

Fighting to hang on, Joe reached in and forced the controls forward. The plane sank back to the earth, its tires barking as they hit the runway.

Holding on to the door frame with one hand, Joe found the back of Mitchell's shirt collar with his other hand and squeezed tight.

Mitchell gasped for air. He took his hands from

the controls and grabbed at Joe's fingers, scraping and prying desperately. Joe just held on tight, choking off Mitchell's air supply. The plane veered off the runway, rattling across a grassy field.

Joe felt Mitchell slump forward. Opening the door, Joe shoved Mitchell aside and settled behind the controls. He brought the flaps up to slow the plane down, then pressed down hard with both feet on the brakes. The plane bounced a few last times, then rolled to a stop.

Joe took a deep breath before radioing the control tower to call the police. By the time he taxied back to PMW, airport security had arrived. Officers were busy loading Pickell into a cruiser and trying to find handcuffs big enough to fit around Buddy's wrists.

"So the crash wasn't Frank's fault," Vanessa said as she and Joe rode the elevator up to Callie's hospital room early the next morning.

"No," Joe said. He balanced a silver tray and lid on his palm like a waiter in a fancy restaurant. "None of the crashes were due to pilot error."

"But how did they fool Hutchens?"

"The plan was fairly simple, actually," Joe said. "Mitchell was regional director down in Louisiana before he came here. He discovered some bad parts at Pickell Machine Works and convinced them that they could make a lot of money selling the stuff they'd normally throw away. All he needed was a mechanic inside the companies to agree to order and install the parts."

"That's where Buddy came in, right?"

Joe watched the elevator light blink from four to five. "Right. He ordered the parts in Ericson's name. Then when the crashes happened, Mitchell would let him into the NTSB hangar to get rid of the evidence."

"And how's Ericson doing?"

The elevator doors opened, and they headed for Callie's room. "He's going to be fine," Joe said. "His only problem was that he was too gung-ho to prove his love for Brenda. He almost got himself killed."

Vanessa elbowed Joe in the ribs. "And what's wrong with that?" she chided.

Joe laughed. "Nothing, I guess. It's just not my style."

"Don't I know it," Vanessa said, holding the door open for Joe. "Here we are."

Inside, they found Frank sitting on the edge of Callie's bed, about to give her a kiss.

"Hold on there, partner," Joe said. "We come with more birthday wishes." He ceremoniously placed the silver tray on Callie's lap and whisked off the lid, revealing a large chocolate cake.

"Thanks, guys," Callie said.

"I know you're not quite well enough to enjoy that yet," Frank said. "But we wanted to celebrate with just the four of us. The party the other night was cut kind of short."

"Oh, you don't get off this easy, Frank Hardy," Callie said. "As soon as I'm better, you're taking me to Loon Lake just like you promised." She smiled. "Just one request, though."

"Name it."

"This time, we drive."

Frank and Joe's next case:

During the early years of World War II, the legendary and lethal Nazi U-boats spread terror from beneath the sea. Now, over fifty years later, on a salvage operation off the coast of Florida, the Hardys plunge into the rusting hull of one of those awesome submarines . . . and discover that the terror still lives! When Alvin Mann, leader of the salvage operation, vanishes without a trace, Frank and Joe vow to rescue him—and find out what deadly secret lies hidden on the ocean bottom. But first they'll have to confront a brutal adversary armed with knives, spearguns, and more—an enemy determined to blow them out of the water . . . in *Dead in the Water,* Case #127 in The Hardy Boys Casefiles™.

THE HARDY BOYS CASEFILES™

- ☐ #1: DEAD ON TARGET 73992-1/$3.99
- ☐ #2: EVIL, INC. 73668-X/$3.99
- ☐ #3: CULT OF CRIME 68726-3/$3.99
- ☐ #14: TOO MANY TRAITORS 73677-9/$3.50
- ☐ #32: BLOOD MONEY 74665-0/$3.50
- ☐ #35: THE DEAD SEASON 74105-5/$3.50
- ☐ #47: FLIGHT INTO DANGER 70044-8/$3.99
- ☐ #49: DIRTY DEEDS 70046-4/$3.99
- ☐ #53: WEB OF HORROR 73089-4/$3.99
- ☐ #54: DEEP TROUBLE 73090-8/$3.99
- ☐ #56: HEIGHT OF DANGER 73092-4/$3.99
- ☐ #57: TERROR ON TRACK 73093-2/$3.99
- ☐ #61: GRAVE DANGER 73097-5/$3.99
- ☐ #65: NO MERCY 73101-7/$3.99
- ☐ #66: THE PHOENIX EQUATION 73102-5/$3.99
- ☐ #72: SCREAMERS 73108-4/$3.75
- ☐ #73: BAD RAP 73109-2/$3.99
- ☐ #75: NO WAY OUT 73111-4/$3.99
- ☐ #76: TAGGED FOR TERROR 73112-2/$3.99
- ☐ #77: SURVIVAL RUN 79461-2/$3.99
- ☐ #78: THE PACIFIC CONSPIRACY 79462-0/$3.99
- ☐ #79: DANGER UNLIMITED 79463-9/$3.99
- ☐ #80: DEAD OF NIGHT 79464-7/$3.99
- ☐ #81: SHEER TERROR 79465-5/$3.99
- ☐ #82: POISONED PARADISE 79466-3/$3.99
- ☐ #83: TOXIC REVENGE 79467-1/$3.99
- ☐ #84: FALSE ALARM 79468-X/$3.99
- ☐ #85: WINNER TAKE ALL 79469-8/$3.99
- ☐ #86: VIRTUAL VILLAINY 79470-1/$3.99
- ☐ #87: DEAD MAN IN DEADWOOD 79471-X/$3.99
- ☐ #88: INFERNO OF FEAR 79472-8/$3.99
- ☐ #89: DARKNESS FALLS 79473-6/$3.99
- ☐ #91: HOT WHEELS 79475-2/$3.99
- ☐ #92: SABOTAGE AT SEA 79476-0/$3.99
- ☐ #93: MISSION: MAYHEM 88204-X/$3.99
- ☐ #94:A TASTE FOR TERROR 88205-8/$3.99
- ☐ #95:ILLEGAL PROCEDURE 88206-6/$3.99
- ☐ #96:AGAINST ALL ODDS 88207-4/$3.99
- ☐ #97:PURE EVIL 88208-2/$3.99
- ☐ #98:MURDER BY MAGIC 88209-0/$3.99
- ☐ #99:FRAME-UP 88210-4/$3.99
- ☐ #100:TRUE THRILLER 88211-2/$3.99
- ☐ #101: PEAK OF DANGER 88212-0/$3.99
- ☐ #102: WRONG SIDE OF THE LAW 88213-9$3.99
- ☐ #103: CAMPAIGN OF CRIME 88214-7$3.99
- ☐ #104: WILD WHEELS 88215-5$3.99
- ☐ #105: LAW OF THE JUNGLE 50428-2$3.99
- ☐ #106: SHOCK JOCK 50429-0/$3.99
- ☐ #107: FAST BREAK 50430-4/$3.99
- ☐ #108: BLOWN AWAY 50431-2/$3.99
- ☐ #109: MOMENT OF TRUTH 50432-0/$3.99
- ☐ #110: BAD CHEMISTRY 50433-9/$3.99
- ☐ #111: COMPETITIVE EDGE 50446-0/$3.99
- ☐ #112: CLIFF-HANGER 50453-3$3.99
- ☐ #113: SKY HIGH 50454-1/$3.99
- ☐ #114: CLEAN SWEEP 50456-8/$3.99
- ☐ #115: CAVE TRAP 50462-2/$3.99
- ☐ #116: ACTING UP 50488-6/$3.99
- ☐ #117: BLOOD SPORT 56117-0/$3.99
- ☐ #118: THE LAST LEAP 56118-9/$3.99
- ☐ #119: THE EMPORER'S SHIELD 56119-7/$3.99
- ☐ #120: SURVIVAL OF THE FITTEST 56120-0/$3.99
- ☐ #121: ABSOLUTE ZERO 56121-9/$3.99
- ☐ #122: RIVER RATS 56123-5/$3.99
- ☐ #123: HIGH-WIRE ACT 56122-7/$3.99
- ☐ #124: THE VIKING'S REVENGE 56124-3/$3.99
- ☐ #125: STRESS POINT 56241-X/$3.99
- ☐ #126: FIRE IN THE SKY 56125-1/$3.99

Simon & Schuster Mail Order
200 Old Tappan Rd., Old Tappan, N.J. 07675

Please send me the books I have checked above. I am enclosing $______(please add $0.75 to cover the postage and handling for each order. Please add appropriate sales tax). Send check or money order--no cash or C.O.D.'s please. Allow up to six weeks for delivery. For purchase over $10.00 you may use VISA: card number, expiration date and customer signature must be included.

Name ____________________

Address ____________________

City ____________________ State/Zip ____________

VISA Card # ____________________ Exp.Date ____________

Signature ____________________ 762-41